Finding Home:

Community in Apocalyptic Worlds

Edited by
Caroline Dombrowski

Presented by
Timid Pirate Publishing

Cover image is by Isobel Craig, "Eggybird." Original work may be found here:
http://www.flickr.com/photos/eggybird/54411097/
Cover itself is copyright Timid Pirate Publishing.

All rights reserved. Each story is copyright © by the author.

No part of this book may be reproduced in any form or by any electronic or mechanical means including information storage and retrieval systems, without permission in writing from the publisher. The only exception is by a reviewer, who may quote short excerpts in a review.

Direct all orders to:
Timid Pirate Publishing
509 N. 85th St. #14,
Seattle, WA 98103
www.timidpirate.com

ISBN 978-0-9830987-7-5
Printed in the United States of America
Timid Pirate Publishing First Edition: December, 2011

All characters in this book are fictitious. Any resemblance to actual apocalypse survivors, living or dead, is purely coincidental.

Dedicated to

The farmers, cob-builders, knife-makers, gardeners, tiny home dwellers and survivors of all kinds.

Special Thanks to
Aarron Kemp, Jennifer Bancroft, Patricia Dombrowski,
Jeremy Matthews, Michaela Hutfles, Isobel Craig
& the Hynes.

Table of Contents

The End
Introduction, by Caroline Dombrowski......................i

Part I. Entrances & Exits
Circulation, by Eric Del Carlo....................................1
My City of Ruins, by Adam Israel 10
Trail of Breadcrumbs, by Jennifer Brozek 21
The Wheel, by Edward Martin III 31
Little Utopia, by Bram E. Gieben 38
Gaia's Legacy, by David Kernot................................51

Part II. The Periphery
Unicorn Chaser, by Minerva Zimmerman 69
Trading with the Ruks, by Nathan Shumate....................89
Midwife, by Jon-Michael Emory.................................95
Girl with Sunrise in her Hair, by Val Muller 105
Forgetfulness, by Dean Kisling 120

Part III. Rule Makers & Breakers
Consensus, by Timons Esaias.....................................133
Maps as Currency, by Melissa Dominic........................142
Aaron's Unmasking, by Chuck Robertson......................156
Affirmations, by S.R. Algernon..................................167
Story, by Butch Kenney..186
How Frank Delano Changed the World, But Not as Much as He Thought, by Torrey Podmajersky......................197
Jar-Washing Day, by Leslie Light...............................202

Aperitif
Lunation, by Michaela Hutfles....................................219

The End.

Now what?

Timid Pirate is full of optimism and joy. Even when we stare directly into the solar flare explosion, tsunami and earthquake news, recessions and ongoing threats of global warming, we shake our heads sadly and then mutter about the thrum of human ingenuity.

When we think of apocalypse, we wonder what we'd do, living in it, later. After the terror. After the demolition. What comes next?

And we see that there will be a "next." Can't keep us humans down. These eighteen stories provide visions and glimpses of futures-that-might-be, of love and building and what happens after "The End."

Dream on.

Caroline Dombrowski

Part I:
Entrances & Exits

Circulation

By
Eric Del Carlo

"You hittin' the road, Grappa?"

It's like a disease we've got, all the old-timers. We don't just remember our taut, energetic youths with heartbreaking clarity. An elder's peculiar grasp of long-term memories gives us the whole scene. We remember the world as it used to be. And as we edge through our winter years, we—almost all of us—start talking about going somewhere. Putting together a boat and cutting away into the waves, filling a canvas with hot air and soaring off over the clouds. Or, more practically, getting some wheels and hitting the road.

I tousle the young'un's fiery red hair, grinning. I'm not his grandfather, nor anybody's. Once, I was quite smug about not breeding, not contributing more humans to what was then (hard to believe) an already overrun planet. My strategy hasn't left me dolefully alone in my dotage. This is a tight-knit community, and everyone loves me. What's not to love? But I share no blood with any of the people around me.

Without answering the boy, I climb my stairs. It's a nice modest tumbledown (soon, literally) house, and every part of it creaks and groans. I've left the motorbike, an ancient algae-burner, out front. Its parts are scattered like a jigsaw, one you don't know if all the pieces are there until you finish—or don't.

But I've got a good feeling about the machine. It's salv given to me for my sixtieth birthday, maybe a gag gift. Back then, "You hittin' the road, Grappa?" would have been asked with irony, and salvaged junk was not intended for use. But I've been working on the bike since, and aggressively these past six months or so.

At the top of my stairs I'm grinning again, but from pain now. Any climb has been tough on my legs for a while, but lately walking on flat ground is rough; and stairs are murder.

I go lie on my musty couch, panting a bit. It hurts to elevate my feet. I dangle them off the edge of the cushions, ungracefully. And wait for the cramps to fade.

* * *

My going causes a big fuss. Some can't believe it, since while people my age talk about it a lot, most don't actually leave. I'm among the doubters, even as I climb onto the saddlebagged bike.

No formal power structure rules the five-hundred strong community which claims this old crumbled town, but our resident spirituality enthusiast, in lieu of any high muckety-muck, shows up for my sendoff. This guy scares me. Not because he is disagreeable in any way; he's a sweet, even-tempered fellow, with a quick mind. But the kids are starting to turn to him with moral and philosophical questions. And he is giving answers. And those answers are just beginning to take on a ritualistic cadence.

I don't listen to his "blessing." I look up at the house where I've lived comfortably for many years. I gaze round at the faces, young and old, every one familiar. Tears are in my eyes, and this whole venture seems astoundingly ridiculous. My calves feel tight, like the flesh is shrinking around the bones.

I fire up the motor. The machine works, and I've already buzzed it back and forth across the town, to everybody's wonder.

Now I hit the throttle, and discover that I really am leaving.

*   *   *

The tangle of off- and on-ramps has been a pile of rubble for twenty years. I have to creep along, navigate mazes of fissures, threading through the dead traffic. Half the time I'm putt-putting along the weedy shoulder. It's good; it keeps me occupied. Otherwise I'd be thinking about turning around, and the final assertive activity of my life would have concluded inside of four hours.

It is as frustrating as a real traffic jam used to be, but, like those, this ordeal eventually ends. I pass the worst onto ever-lengthening clear stretches. Erosion has done a hell of a number on the road surfaces, of course, but the motorbike is maneuverable and I'm not hurrying. Even so, the speeds I do hit are exhilarating.

More than my legs hurt. My back throbs, my shoulder joints are making themselves painfully known, and I am sweating like a pig under this leather jacket I dug out from the depths of my belongings. But I press on, feeling something close to giddiness.

The clot of decaying coastal cities starts to recede behind me. I am taken into the network of ancient concrete arteries that once pumped through this land.

*   *   *

Soil has rolled in, and grass sprung up. But mostly I can still follow the roads. There are even long, flat distances where phone poles still stand, strung stubbornly with inert cable. I twist the bike's throttle and go flinging along, wind raking my hair. Well, what hair I've got. My scalp is a bit sunburned because I couldn't find a helmet, but screw it—no pussy helmet laws anymore, anyway.

I had a cycle when I was young—when I was a boy, it feels like now. Amazing how every bit of it has come back to me. I handle the seaweed-burner like I've taken a month off from riding. The machine hums and jounces as the front wheel parts the grass like the prow of a speedboat. The balance feels right. I'm joined to the bike.

But I also feel connected to the landscape I'm passing through. That was always the difference between going by two wheels rather than four. In a car, you would miss most of what was happening around you. It was like watching a travel TV show instead of actually traveling.

I bet I've gone a hundred miles in three days. That is, simply, astonishing. I try to imagine telling that to the kid with the fiery red hair, the one who lived on my block. He would look up at me, wide-eyed, slack-jawed, uncomprehending. What's Grappa talking about?

In the late afternoon, I camp. I don't let myself miss my bed too much. The tent is cozy, the sleeping bag comfortable. I build a fire as night comes, not because it's cold, but because it seems the thing to do. This is my life now, what I'm going to do with what I've got left. It was the right move. I am not just saying that until it sticks. On a deep level, I truly feel it.

I eat sparingly from my supplies, but enjoy the tastes, more than I usually do. This adventure seems to be sharpening my senses.

Finally, though, I have to undo my jeans and awkwardly shimmy them down to the tops of my boots. I knead at my thighs and check the ulcers—there are two now—by the firelight. There is no white-coated medical professional to sling a word like "claudication" at me, but that's what it is: vascular disease. Arteries have had enough of schlepping my blood. They want a day off but can't have one, so they dog it. I am not bitter about it. I'm tired too.

I am sitting there before my fire, in half-naked view—somehow it figures—when the woman steps in out of the night.

She says, "Hi. I saw your fire."

Surprise, fear and embarrassment jolt me, and I make it worse by trying to hop to my feet and rake my jeans up. My hopping days are behind me, and I nearly stumble headlong into my fire. My brain is trying to react a dozen different ways; I flash on where my hunting knife is (in one of the saddlebags) and where my bike sits in relation to this woman (she is a few steps to the left of being directly between me and it). But I also note that she has spoken in a friendly manner and her hands are empty.

So the surprise passes with that first surge of adrenaline, the fear starts to ease as I assess my visitor, and I'm left with the mortification of getting caught with my pants down—so very literally.

There are a lot of things I could say, but I employ the simplest. "Hi."

She is young. Then again, my definition of young has changed with each successive decade. She's probably thirty, maybe a year or two more, but that's still much too young to have been around when the electrical grid went down for the last time; too young even for those wild years that followed, the ones I could never talk about, at least not with anyone who wasn't also there.

So, she is young. And alone.

Or, at least, no one else has come into the light.

"Strange," I hear myself say. "I never thought about meeting anybody out here."

She smiles. There is no sign that she's embarrassed by my state of undress. "Well, here I am. I was just rolling by..." She nods over her shoulder.

Another vehicle! I didn't even hear it come up. So much for my sharpened senses. The crackle of the fire, my preoccupation with examining my legs—but really it's just that I don't hear so well anymore.

Her cycle is parked a short ways from mine, about forty yards off the grassy strip that was U.S. Route number-something-or-other once. Her machine looks cobbled together, like mine.

I meant to take a strictly solitary journey. I wasn't even going to go near any old population centers. I barely remember how to deal with a stranger, after living so long in an isolated, insular community. And surely the rules are different now.

But, again, I go the simplest way. "My name's Cam."

"Cam?"

"Cameron."

"I'm named Janey."

Maybe I expected some weird tribal name, but I'm relieved that it's so ordinary.

Finding Home

"You want to come sit at my fire?" I offer. Again, it just seems like the thing to do. Some urge toward civilized hospitality, maybe.

"Purple," Janey says, and comes to sit.

I blink at the non sequitur. She said it like you'd say "Thanks" or "Cool."

She dips a hand into her jacket—an old battered leather, much like mine—and I tense again. But she comes out with a small plastic canteen. "Want some?" There is no guile in her voice or demeanor. She hands it across the fire.

I sniff, I sip and taste a sweet liquor, with just enough sting to tell me it is newly fermented. Whoever Janey is, she is no road marauder, or any other fanciful post-apocalyptic archetype. She's just a woman, a person, and she is sharing her booze the way I share my fire.

After knocking back a bigger swallow, I give her back the canteen, and she drinks too, without wiping the spout. Maybe this is some…ritual?

"That's a nice-looking bike," Janey says.

For the first time I hear an accent, a musical twang that's maybe cracker mixed with Spanish, but still with no hint of a threat. "Yours too," I say, a little awed at how automatic my reply is, as if the polite repartee is some race memory I have been carrying from the old days. But she has the same manners. Where did she learn them?

I look beyond the dancing yellow flames, which give Janey's dark hair a golden shine. My sight is a lot better than my hearing. I'm gazing beyond her cycle now, at the open land sprinkled with star- and moonlight, but there's still nobody moving, no confederates closing in. With all the salv that must be available out here, it is hard to imagine a need for waylaying or thieving, but you never know.

Until, I decide, I do know. She is alone and friendly, and making civil overtures. Her alcohol has spread warmth through my chest and even eased the throbbing of my legs a bit. I smile at her, and she smiles again at me.

We start in talking about motorbikes, and all follows from there. That, I suddenly remember, is the key to strangers: find a single commonality; after that, the strangeness becomes familiar.

Once, long ago, I would have tried talking to her about baseball or movies or—last resort—politics.

But inside ten minutes we're pals, and pals tell each other things. She tells me, "We've been doing this for—let's see. Two months now. We got an old woman, round your age, used to be a mechanic. She keeps building the cycles out of parts. We had to do something with them."

"So you've gone exploring." I shake my head in wonder, imagining the fleet of motorbikes departing, fanning out across the land. But that is also a troubling image, and it takes me a moment to figure out why.

Janey says proudly, "We've sent out at least twenty scouts by now, going every which way."

I eye her. She's not unattractive, but I don't let that distract me. "And what," I ask, "is the plan? The ultimate plan, I mean. Your group—your community, your tribe, whatever—you're going to get everybody…organized? You got somebody back home who wants to be a leader?"

I am surprised at the vehemence in my voice, but she just blinks, nonplussed.

I do, however, understand my own aversion to power structures, to hierarchies. After all, I have seen the biggest system of all fail in spectacular, supreme, catastrophic fashion. The idea of starting it up again, even on a crude level, curdles me.

But Janey shrugs, and says, "We just want to meet other people. Talk. Trade ideas. It's just…travel. Movement. Where I grew up," she nods over her shoulder again, vaguely to the east over the onetime Nevada border, "we were…I don't know. Starting to get stale, I think. No new thoughts. And one or two of us—. Maybe some of us did want to be leaders. But I don't want to be led. Do you?"

"Hell, no." Then, thinking of the spiritually-minded fellow back in my town, I add, "Leaders and oracles lead to ceremonies and dogma. Or maybe it's the other way round. Either, it's the start of mindlessness, of obedience, of subservience."

Am I talking over her head? Maybe. But I am certain I could make her understand, and that she would agree.

"How 'bout you?" she asks. She has the plastic flask in hand again; she sips, and passes it over. "What are you doing out here?"

I almost don't say. But we're pals now. So I tell her. My throat chokes some. I hope the firelight doesn't pick up the shine in my eyes. I finish talking about gangrene and what I'll eventually have to use the hunting knife for. It's not to perform a self-amputation; I'm a lot less heroic than that.

I take a big swallow of her booze. Again, I feel the warmth, but there is also relief spreading through me. Relief at what this woman doesn't represent, relief to have told her what I didn't tell anybody back home. I meant this to be my terminal ride. Now, maybe, I can do something else with this last part of my life.

Janey comes around the fire and hugs me. She is completely unself-conscious about it, which tells me something about wherever she is from.

She asks, "So, what do you want to do?"

I understand the two choices, though I could ignore them both if I wanted and just continue on like I originally intended.

I say, "Take me to your people." Rather than: I'll take you to mine. I want a look at her home before I tell her where my own community is. Might as well be smart if I'm going to take on this duty.

"Purple." A grin replaces her smile.

"Purple, indeed," I agree. New ways. New ideas. She was right: it is all about movement.

She camps with me. We'll head east in the morning. It takes me quite a while to fall asleep, long after Janey is softly murmuring in her own sleeping bag. As a treat, I let myself wonder about the older female mechanic who built those cycles.

Her I want to meet.

Eric Del Carlo's short fiction has appeared in *Strange Horizons*, *Futurismic*, *Talebones* and many other venues. He has work upcoming at *Asimov's* and *Redstone Science Fiction*. In addition to short stories, he has co-authored several novels with the late Robert Asprin, including a New Orleans murder mystery entitled *NO Quarter* published by DarkStar Books. On his own, he has written novels and novellas for Loose Id and Ravenous Romance. In 2005, he fled New Orleans a day ahead of Hurricane Katrina and has since resettled in his native California. For contact or more info, check out ericdelcarlo.com.

My City of Ruins
(It Shall Rise Again)

By
Adam Israel

Detroit leaned forward and turned off the recorder, ending another message that would never be sent home. The scavenger's autopilot beeped steadily, following the radio beacon from Cleveland. The 360° showed a total whiteout but it'd been that way since he passed through Akron.

Faint heat signatures were noticeable on the infrared ahead, where a bay door opened to meet him. The throttle eased, letting the treads fall one by one until the nose of the cab kissed the inside wall and the clearance light signaled green. The autopilot disengaged, and the scavenger fell idle.

As expected, the first people he saw were dockworkers. They smiled and waved as they approached, and Detroit unlocked the latches securing the cargo before disembarking.

Detroit's skin prickled when he stepped away from his home and into the warehouse. The air was cold but fresher than anything he'd tasted in weeks. Aside from the smell of cured meat and body odor, the scavenger's air recycler was efficient; it kept him warm and he was more grateful for that every day he pushed further north.

"Welcome to Cleveland, sir," one of the dockworkers said. "Follow the arrows to the office."

The heels of his boots thudded as he walked deeper into the warehouse, passing empty bays or jerrybuilt vehicles that he wouldn't have trusted with his life on a sunny day before the freeze. There was no sign of their pilots, or anyone else, when the arrow dead-ended at a large waiting area.

"Detroit?"

Detroit spun around, surprised by the sound of the familiar voice. There'd been a half dozen of them, young men from across the country and it'd been just as easy to remember where they were from as it was their given names.

The likeness of the man standing of the doorway took him back nearly a decade. The shape of his face was the same, but its surface bore the same scars Detroit's did when he looked in the mirror—wrinkles that sprawled endlessly, bags that hung around like bad memories, no matter how much you tried to forget. Time and the harsh cycle of life had not been kind to either of them.

"Cleve? Is that really you?"

The man stepped forward. They shook hands, hesitating briefly on protocol, then embraced each other as only old friends could.

"Aren't you a sight. When I heard my dispatcher trying to describe that vehicle, I knew it had to be you. How'd you convince them to let you keep it?"

"It wasn't too hard. I was running relief supplies out of Atlanta after the first freeze. Word came in about casualties and we had some real unrest. Morale broke. Men up and left their posts."

"Did your family make it out…" Cleveland said.

"No," he interrupted. "They were still in Detroit."

"I'm sorry, man."

Detroit shrugged, pretending apathy. "It's about survival now, right?"

"Looks like you're doing pretty alright for yourself. That haul you brought in is more than we've seen in a month."

"Scrap, mostly, pickings from the dead," he said. "There's just not enough stuff to go around."

"About that," Cleveland said. "How about you come have supper with me and the family and let me make you a crazy proposal. Besides, you smell like you could use a shower."

* * *

Detroit throttled up the engines of the scavenger, putting distance between himself and Cleveland. The rumble of the treads over the ten-foot thick sheet of ice blanketing Lake Erie didn't do much to distract him from where he was heading. Cleveland's suggestion to go north to salvage the equipment his factories needed to build better transportation was logical. Detroit's hometown was an untapped resource of materials that no one, living or dead, would complain about missing, and his scavenger was built to work in the kind of conditions found there. It would be years before any kind of organized recovery effort reached this far north, if one ever did.

All Detroit had to do was enter the city of the dead, confront the ghosts of his past and salvage the skeleton of the city he loved.

The lake was a desolate wasteland filled with the same stark white landscape; the hundred-mile stretch of winding river leading north wasn't much better. The Ambassador Bridge, linking Detroit to Windsor, materialized in the distance around mid-afternoon. Everything about the city looked like a mirage, with its ice-covered buildings and the strange purple haze in the sky above, until he reached the waterfront. He made landfall downtown, where a makeshift ramp had been built and fresh tracks cut through the fresh snow.

The thermal scanner couldn't find any heat signatures, but they were only so effective under the extreme conditions. He pushed the scavenger ahead, through the heart of Detroit's downtown, loud and slow. If he couldn't find whoever had made those tracks, he'd make sure they found him.

It didn't take long. A few minutes later, a pair of snowmobiles with metal canopies protecting the drivers crossed his path ahead and came to a stop. He tried to slow, but the scavenger lurched to a stop. Lights flashed in the cabin, warning of debris in the treads.

This close to the aurora, the radio played nothing but a pitchy wail. The snowmobiles idled, as if waiting for him to do something. Detroit punched up the scanners, to see if there was anything he was missing. Faint heat signatures, mostly from the exhaust pipes, and there, a distinct blinking pattern in a rear taillight. Brilliant. They were using it as a heliograph to communicate.

The communication system was smart enough to translate, once he told it what to look for. After a few minutes, the computer's synthetic voice filled the cabin.

"Who are you and what the hell are you doing?"

"Leroy Kilpatrick," Detroit said, "former Army Specialist, Resurrection Company, 43rd Armored Division, Salvage and Transport."

"US Army?"

Detroit leaned back in his chair, mulling over the ramifications of the question. Everything he thought he knew, everything they told him, was wrong. "Of course US Army. Who else?"

"Raiders from across the river. Needed to be sure. What took you so long?"

Detroit's heart sank. No one else knew that there were survivors. They had all been left to fend for themselves since the freeze, and it sounded like their hopes were pinned on a rescue party of one.

"I don't know," he said, "we didn't know anyone north of the, well, the kill line survived."

"Aren't many of us, but those that did survive are inland. There are co-ops spread throughout the suburbs but the big enclave is in Dearborn, due west about ten miles. They'll be eager for news from the south."

"As soon as I find my family. You have my word."

"Erm, about your treads. When we thought you were from cross-river, we clogged them with a plastic glue polymer. You'll need to cut your way free."

It'd been too long since Detroit had an excuse to stretch his legs and he always liked to put on a show. He climbed through the hatch at the rear of the cab and strapped himself in. The engines powered up when he gripped the controls.

"That won't be a problem," he relayed through the comm link with the scavenger before undocking from berth. Arms unlocked and extended, the body rose, and the head popped up, a bit like a jack in a box.

The first few seconds of flight were unsteady, while thrusters warmed up and melted away accumulated ice but the sight of the scavenger's built-in power suit taking flight always got their attention.

* * *

The city of Detroit spread out for miles in every direction, a frozen wonderland of urban sprawl. From his birds' eye view, Detroit could imagine the city as it used to be, veins leading from the heart of downtown to carry life to far suburban corners. From this height, nothing else moved. The arteries were clogged and the body died with it, but pockets of life survived within the decay.

He flew north, low over the skyline, towards the quiet subdivision they moved to a month before his last redeployment orders came in. A small neighborhood, close to his parents, so Lashawna could save money on daycare. Now the houses were frozen, in time and memory. He had to know for sure.

The car, a burgundy minivan bought with his dad's employee discount, still parked in the driveway. The windows were too dark to see through, so he punched through them and flipped on the floodlights. The vehicle was empty.

The mech's biofeedback monitor beeped in his helmet, warning him that his vitals were spiking, but he didn't care. The mech was built for cutting things apart and that's what he meant to do. He ignited all six carving lasers and, wielding them like a samurai warrior, began cutting into their dream home.

Detroit cut his way from top to bottom, shredding drywall and wood like tissue paper. He found pictures and mementos, baby toys, and his wife's wedding dress hanging in their closet, all ruined by the freeze. The only sign of Lashawna or his baby girl were the dirty dishes frozen in a block of dishwater.

His parents' house told the same story from the outside, with one car parked in the driveway but the front door stood open. He made short work of removing the front wall, revealing a scene of horror. The card table was set up in the living room, cards dealt among cups of coffee and plates of donuts. The ladies of his mother's afternoon bridge club, gathered for the last time.

Detroit switched off the speaker blaring in his ears as he looked upon the face of the woman who raised him. She survived growing up in the inner city, a car accident that cost her foot, and two bouts of cancer. He'd thought she was invincible. At least, judging by the expressions on their faces, they went happy. That's how she would have wanted it.

Amber light flashed inside his helmet. He flipped the audio back on and the biofeedback warnings were replaced by a new threat. The mech was running on reserves. He had to say goodbye and get back to the scavenger before his suit ran out of power and he became a part of this place's history, too.

Dusk had fallen by the time he returned downtown. He snaked an auxiliary cable from the mech's storage bay and plugged in with minutes to spare.

Under the haze of the aurora, he burned the welcoming party's polymer away from the treads and settled in for the night.

* * *

Finding Home

Most of the cars on the westbound interstate leaving the city had been cleared, giving Detroit a clear path to drive. He was five miles outside the city, making good time, when a single retrofitted snowmobile pulled out on the road from an off-ramp. The driver, obviously surprised by the sight of the scavenger in his rearview mirror, darted like a startled jackrabbit up the next ramp.

Detroit hammered his foot on the brake and veered right, barely making the exit in time. He opened the throttle as he rounded the curve, catching sight of his prey as it made another turn. Its exhaust pipe burned white on the infrared, making it easy to spot. All he had to do was keep up.

The chase led him through several neighborhoods he vaguely remembered, past shopping malls, empty storefronts and husks of buildings. Not much about the place had changed, all things considered. It wasn't until they neared an industrial district that the landscape changed. The normally blue infrared field glowed with specks of reds and oranges coming from buildings.

The jackrabbit skidded around a corner and out of sight, but the familiar silhouette of twin brick smokestacks billowing smoke caught Detroit's attention and he skidded to a stop across from the building. Individual flares of yellow and white on his monitor were unmistakable, but blurred together, making it impossible to tell how many people were inside. Someone was running his father's factory. He climbed into the mech and prepared to knock on the front door.

Halfway across the field leading to the building, the thrusters sputtered. Detroit triggered the controls to run a diagnostic. For a brief moment the heads up display flickered, every indicator dangerously close to redlining, before going dark.

The mech lost power and entered free fall.

Thousands of pounds of machine and man connected with the ground with a crunch.

* * *

Detroit dreamt that he was at the beach, swimming in the warm, salty water. Waves washed over his body and the wind's fingers ran through his hair. He tried to open his eyes and the bright light burned his eyes even in the idyllic vision.

"Wake up, sunshine."

Detroit sat up so fast that the room seemed to spin around him. He lay in a bath of warm blue gel, and every muscle in his body hurt. He took in details by turn, the starkness of the room, the faint smell of grease and the man standing behind him.

"Dad?"

The smile was almost as wide as his face. "It's good to see you, son. We'd lost hope that you'd find us."

"I didn't know. We lost most everything north of the 42nd. Russia, northern Europe, Britain, Canada. They said there was no hope."

The old man was silent while he helped Detroit to his feet and handed him dry clothes—a dark blue mechanic's jumpsuit. Tears welled in his eyes.

"Lashawna? The baby?" Detroit said.

"Lashawna and Aisha are fine. Your mom…" His voice trailed off.

"I know," Detroit interrupted, wrapping his arms around his father. "I should have been here. I'm so sorry."

"Nonsense," the man said. "You had a job to do and no one blames you for not being here."

"I do," Detroit said. "Everything was falling apart and I didn't know if I could face what I expected to find. I only came because I ran out of excuses. It was time to help someone other than myself."

"Let it go, son. You're here now. That's what matters."

Lashawna opened the door, Aisha in tow.

"There'll be plenty of time for that later, son. First, I think someone is here to see you."

He recognized the tightness in his wife's face, the need to see for herself, that eased when their eyes met, Whatever happened next, Detroit knew that everything was going to be alright.

* * *

Detroit and family followed his father through the factory. Men and women at their stations, sweat dripping from the heat of the forge and muscles bulging under the strain of work.

"Infrastructure is critical. Refiring that," his father said, pointing to the forge in the center of the room, "was our top priority. We had metal workers, electrical workers, autoworkers… it all sort of came together. We piped the excess heat underground through old sewer lines and into nearby buildings. We have living space and factories all over town."

"What are you building?"

"We've learned a thing or two about adapting to the cold. You've seen our snowmobiles. Those are assembled across town. We make the weather-resistant plating here. That lets us transport goods between the other co-ops."

The scavenger was parked on a loading dock, its door slightly ajar. The remains of the mech, badly dented, lay in its bed.

"One of the men has some, ah, skill in picking locks and thought it safer to bring it inside."

"So this is where you lived?" Lashawna said, squeezing his hand.

"It wasn't so bad, once I got used to it. I recorded most of my messages home from up front."

"Messages?"

"Oh," he said. "When I didn't think I'd see you again, I recorded videos to you and Aisha."

Detroit climbed up and reached behind the driver's seat. He didn't have many personal effects. He'd kept one special package tucked away in case of a miracle.

His daughter was still in diapers the last time he saw her. Now she walked and talked. She stood behind Lashawna, head resting to her mother's hip, waiting shyly as if unsure of what to make of this strange man she only knew from pictures and stories. If they had told her about him at all, he realized.

Detroit knelt down in front of his daughter, trying to ignore the stiffness in his joints. She reacted by clenching her mother's leg protectively. "Hi, sweetheart. I brought this a long way, just for you," he said, offering her the package, wrapped in colorful old paper.

The girl looked to her mother and grandfather for approval. Receiving nods from both, she reached out and snatched the gift from Detroit's hands. They watched as she ripped at the paper, torn bits drifting to the floor.

The teddy bear was custom-made before the freeze, complete with fatigues and his name stitched across the vest. It was meant as a birthday present, more than three years ago. She laughed with delight and hugged her new best friend, the gleam in her eyes all the thanks he could have asked for.

Detroit stood and dabbed at his eyes with his sleeve. This family reunion amid the sparks of machinery, metal and the heat of the forge was the most cherished event in his life.

His father's hand fell on his shoulder. "She'll come around, son," he said quietly. "She was just a baby. It'll just take some time for her to adjust."

* * *

A dozen men and women sat in chairs or slouched in corners of darkened reception area, with the occasional snore slipping loose.

It didn't take long for a familiar face to find his way to greet them, hair jumbled from sleep. "Detroit? What the hell? You were supposed to be back with that equipment six months ago. I thought you were dead. Again."

Detroit embraced the befuddled man. "It's good to see you too, Cleveland."

The other drivers were filing in. There weren't enough docks to hold all of the newly built vehicles Detroit brought with him.

"Who are all these people?"

"Friends and family," he said, grinning. "There are survivors in the north. Tens of thousands, alive and thriving. We brought a fleet of transports with us, ready to do business."

Cleveland's mouth dropped open.

"Materials and the equipment you'll need for construction," Detroit said, "plus a few dozen weathered snowmobiles for moving around at a distance safely."

He could see the Cleveland thinking. This was much bigger than the salvage operation they had discussed. "What's the catch?"

"Consider it a down payment."

"On what, exactly?"

Detroit grinned. "Logistics. I have contacts from New Pittsburg to Atlanta. Do you still have yours in Indianapolis, Memphis, and Dallas?"

Cleveland nodded. "Sure do."

"Good. Let's stop living piecemeal. What say we build ourselves a trade network?"

Adam Israel was born in northern Illinois, and has since lived and worked in the suburbs of Chicago, New York City, and Los Angeles. He is now an expatriate living in southwest Ontario, Canada with his wife, three dogs, and three cats, hardly a stone's throw away from where much of this story takes place.

Adam has worked as a secretary, a messenger, a forklift driver, a welder, a fry slinger, and as a cleaner in a slaughterhouse. Now he divides his time between freelance software engineering and writing. A 2010 graduate of the Clarion Writers Workshop, Adam is a regular contributor to the Inkpunks group blog (www.inkpunks.com) and occasionally updates his own website at www.adamisrael.com.

A Trail of Breadcrumbs

By
Jennifer Brozek

Am I brave enough to make the trip? That's what I wondered a month ago. Two weeks ago, I decided I was. Four hundred and thirty miles is nothing. Eight hours in a car. No problems.

Right.

Eight hours in a car and four hundred and thirty miles... If a bunch of the roads aren't blocked. By freeway. If you can use all of the freeway. If you go the speed limit and not the twenty to thirty miles an hour because you're too afraid of crashing into an abandoned car or some other bit of rubble. If the end of the world hadn't come in the form of plague and mother nature just months ago.

It's been six hours and I just now got to the I-205 exit to go around Vancouver and Portland. The roads are mostly clear outside the big cities. Mostly. I almost crashed into an 18-wheeler about an hour back. That woke me up for sure.

No. I haven't seen anyone else alive. A lot of rotting corpses, yes. Living people, no.

I'm not going to make it to Grants Pass tonight. I might not make it for another week if I'm lucky.

Wait. What's that? What the hell?

* * *

Finding Home

Kayley slammed on her brakes and skidded to a stop before the sign. In two foot high, bright orange letters on wood was her name, with an arrow pointing towards the exit she was about to pass. She stared at it for a long time. Then she put the jeep in gear, got off the freeway and headed into Vancouver.

The roads had the look of a town that had tried to keep its streets clear but failed in the end. No faster than twenty miles an hour, Kayley turned from one main street to another and then to a smaller neighborhood street until she was deep into the Walnut Grove area of Vancouver. Each turn was heralded by an orange-lettered sign with her name and an arrow. As trails of breadcrumbs go, this one was very clear.

Each turn made her heart pound harder in her chest and Kayley was sure her tongue would have been stuck to the roof of her mouth if she hadn't been panting. This realization made her stop the jeep and work to get control of herself. Until then, she did not know she could both panic and be overly excited at the same time.

"It's ok. It's ok," she whispered to herself. "They want me here. If they're still alive. It may be nothing. You've got to prepare yourself for that."

The sound of her own voice soothed her. Between her iPod and her portable DVD player, Kayley was still used to the sound of other people's voices and talking to herself…or back to the movie she was playing. It was her coping mechanism. She took a couple more deep breaths. "If it is someone, we'll deal with it. It'll be ok."

It dismayed her how frightened she was.

With one last deep breath, Kayley put the jeep in gear again and followed the breadcrumbs home.

* * *

Home turned out to be nice, two story white house on a corner with a three-car garage. The yard was meticulously neat—strangely so, compared to the months of growth in nearby yards. The house had a "Kayley! Please Knock!" sign in the well-trimmed front yard. On the covered porch, it looked like a teenage girl had died against the front door. *Locked out of the house forever,* Kayley thought with a pang. She had seen a lot of bodies but this one hurt because it had been waiting for her.

Then the body moved. The girl stood up and stepped to the edge of the porch, watching her.

Alive.

The girl was alive!

For a moment, the two of them stared at each other across the yard. Kayley smiled and unbuckled her seatbelt. She opened the jeep door and slid to the yard. The girl had taken two steps closer and they stared at each other across the hood of the jeep.

Finally, Kayley said, "I, uh, followed your signs."

"Kayley?"

Kayley nodded, unable to say anything.

"I'm Emily." She paused. "You came."

"I guess I did."

"What took you so long?"

It was the kind of question a teenager would ask. "I had to get my head wrapped around the idea that the end had come. How'd you know I'd drive this way?"

Emily smiled, "I knew you lived in Redmond. So, I put signs on both I-5 and 205. I wasn't sure which way you'd come."

"You knew I lived in Redmond?"

"Uh, yeah. It's not like it was secret. It was on your blog after all. Young, not stupid."

Kayley nodded, "Sorry, it surprised me."

"And you're older than I thought you'd be. What are you, like, thirty?"

"Twenty-two! What are you? Twelve?"

"Thirteen!"

The two of them looked at each other for a moment before bursting out into peals of laughter. Somehow, they crossed the distance between them and were hugging, laughing, and babbling at each other. The laughter would die down, they'd look at each other, and it would start up again.

But Kayley could hear the hysterical edge on Emily's laughter. In the blink of an eye, Emily was hugging her in a fierce grip and crying. "You finally came. You finally came," she sobbed into Kayley's arms.

All Kayley could do for the moment was hold her, pet her hair, and murmur soothing words over and over.

* * *

It took about ten minutes to get Emily calmed down enough to get her into the house. Then Kayley distracted her by asking how she kept things so neat (regular chores), how she put up the signs (moped) and where she got her electricity (generator but only when really needed). Soon, they decided that it was time for dinner.

Emily made Kayley sit at the kitchen table while she worked. "This is my house, after all."

"You've done really well for yourself," Kayley said. "Better than me, I think."

"Wasn't that hard. Daddy was in the military. We all had some sort of training for emergencies. I guess I learned more than I thought."

"I guess you did." She watched as Emily moved about the kitchen, out the back door to start the generator, and into the pantry. "I think a lot of people could learn something from watching you."

Emily shrugged. "Maybe." She didn't look up from the fresh vegetables as she diced. "What are you going to do now?"

"Eat an amazing dinner, first. Fresh veggies!"

"I know. I didn't think I'd miss them until they were gone. I have a little garden out back." She paused, "And you know that's not what I mean."

Kayley nodded. "I know. I'm not really sure." She thought about all of those side streets she did not take and wondered if she had missed people along the way. She wondered if she should go back or first to Grants Pass and then back again.

"You could stay here with me."

Kayley looked at her, the idea enticing, and then shook her head, "I can't do that, hon. I promised… I promised I'd go to Grants Pass." She saw Emily's face fall and quickly added, "But, you could come with me, if you like."

* * *

While they ate, Emily talked about her life before and after T.E. "The End. Because, that's what it was. My family did pretty well. At first, anyway. None of them got sick. Then, one day, Mom, Dad and Nick were sick. Three days later, they were all dead. There was no one to help me bury the bodies. There were people around, but they didn't want to come anywhere near me. I might be catching. Like Typhoid Mary."

Emily played with her food as she talked.

Kayley let her say what she needed to say and didn't interrupt.

"Maybe I am. They got sick and died and I didn't. At first, I cried a lot. Then I did what Dad and Mom taught me to do in a crisis—hunker down and survive. We had a lot of food and water here. Dad wouldn't let the stocks dwindle or go bad. Changed the water out every six months and stuff."

Emily stabbed a carrot with her fork and held it up for inspection. "Then I realized that I hadn't heard or seen a person for three days. I moved from hunkered down to looking around and those who hadn't left were dead. Do you know how weird it is to go into your neighbor's house without permission?"

Kayley nodded with a knowing smile.

"I thought it would feel naughty. Like I was getting away with something. Instead, it felt blasphemous…like I was trespassing on holy ground. So weird." She shook her head. "In any case, I cleared the neighborhood of bodies that were outside. I didn't want coyotes or dogs to get to them. I don't think I could've handled that."

Emily ate the carrot. "Once that was done, I fixed up the place and added the garden. I was bored a lot without TV and stuff. It worked out. Except, I kinda miss butter. I haven't figured out how to do any of that or where to get a cow."

Kayley chuckled. "I don't know if there are cows in Grants Pass but I've got a great series of books that will help with that. I miss butter, too."

"What books?"

"The Foxfire series. They're going to help us rebuild some semblance of civilization once we're settled in."

Emily nodded. "Butter would be nice."

* * *

The strawberry PopTart was cold, far too sweet, and still wonderful. For sleeping on the couch, Kayley felt good. "Once we make it to Grants Pass, we'll look around, see if there are people and if there are, we'll go from there."

Emily nodded as she picked the crust off her blueberry PopTart and broke up the rest into bite-sized pieces.

"If there aren't any people. Well, I guess we can either continue to head south before the winter hits or we can come back here. We'll have to decide at the time. One thing I've learned in this new world is you can never be sure of your plans but it is always good to have some."

Emily nodded again, breaking the pieces of pop tart into even smaller bites.

Kayley frowned, realizing that Emily had neither said a word nor eaten anything since they got up. "What's wrong?"

"I'm not coming." Emily did not look up.

"What?"

"I'm not coming with you to Grants Pass."

Kayley stared at her for a long time, "Why not?"

Emily looked at Kayley. Fear was etched all over her face. "This is my home. I can't go. This is where my parents are buried."

"But…"

Emily stood and walked over to the counter, "It was easy for you to leave Redmond. You didn't have a family there. You hadn't even settled into a permanent place. This is my home."

"It wasn't easy! It took me months to get up the courage to come." Kayley stood and walked over to her. "Please, come with me." It was easier to plead to the teenager's back.

"You could stay."

"I can't."

"You could."

"If I had stayed in Redmond, I would never have found you. Who else is waiting for me?"

"Does it matter? What if no one is there?"

Kayley stepped back. "Yeah. It matters." She turned away and started gathering her things. "I have to go. I promised."

Emily turned on her. "Who? Who did you promise?"

Kayley sighed. "You remember when I made that blog post fourteen months ago? The one that told everyone to meet me in Grants Pass when the end of the world came?"

"Yeah."

"That's what I promised you and everyone else who is still alive. I didn't know I was making a promise. I didn't know the end of the world would come. It was a whimsical thought. But the end did come and the blog post did become a promise."

Emily stared at her, fists clenched.

"I have to go." Kayley said, her voice soft. She watched Emily for a long moment before she slung her pack over her shoulder and walked to the front door. "Are you sure you won't come with me?"

Emily shook her head. "*This* is my home."

Kayley nodded. "All right. Whether or not there's anyone at Grants Pass, I will come back. If there's someone there, I'll come get you. If no one's there, I'll come back here." She opened the front door. "Then I'll decide what to do." She walked out the door, leaving it open behind her. Every step away from Emily broke her heart. Kayley wanted to stay but Emily's very existence proved that she had to go.

Kayley paused at the jeep door and looked back. "Come with me." Her voice was soft but it carried on the wind.

Emily, in the doorway, walked out to the edge of the porch, "Stay." Her voice was just as soft and pleading.

Kayley shook her head. "Ok. I'll be back. Two or three weeks if all goes well." She paused, but Emily did not say anything and there was nothing holding her back. Kayley swung herself into the jeep, started it up, and pulled away.

Emily did not move.

Kayley wanted her to run after the jeep, to give her a reason to stop, and still Emily did not move. Then she was around the corner and Emily was out of sight.

* * *

Twenty minutes later, Kayley sat on the freeway onramp arguing with herself. After a fierce battle within, she sighed and muttered, "I hate being the grownup." She started up the jeep again, turned it around, and followed the signs back to Emily's house.

Emily was there on the steps of the porch with her face in her hands.

Kayley got out of the jeep and marched over to the girl. "All right, young lady…"

Emily looked up, her face was puffy, red and wet from her tears, "You left me!"

"You let me leave!" Kayley shouted back.

Emily stood, "You left!"

"I came back!"

That deflated Emily's rage and fear, "You came back."

"Yes. Now, you're going to go get that bag I know you packed last night and you're going to put it in the jeep. Then we're going to go to Grants Pass to see what's there. Then, we'll see what we do next."

"You're not my mom." Emily's voice took on a more familiar and comfortable surly teenage tone.

"No. I'm not your mom. But I'm the only grownup you've got. Now get moving, young lady."

Emily paused, looking like she was going to argue more, then she turned around and walked back into the house.

"Chop-chop. We've got miles to go before dark," Kayley called after her.

A couple minutes later, Emily reappeared with two suitcases. She also had a shotgun slung over one shoulder and a pistol at her waist. Kayley reached for one of the suitcases to help. It was heavy.

"Oof! What do you have in here? A ton of bricks?"

"My whole life," Emily said, her voice subdued.

Kayley looked at her and saw that she meant it. "Ok, then. We'll make it fit in the back."

Once they were both settled into the jeep, Emily armed with the most recent Thomas Guides Kayley could find, Kayley looked at her and asked, "Ready?"

Emily nodded and then admitted, "Ready, but scared."

"Me, too. But at least we won't have to face it alone."

* * *

Am I brave enough to make the trip? That's what I wondered a month ago. Now, with Emily beside me, I wonder if I'm brave enough for the two of us. I think I am.

There's something about having another person to care for, argue with and depend on that makes you more than you are.

It's two hundred and fifty miles or so from here to Grants Pass. I don't know what or who we'll encounter along the way. Like Emily says, I'm ready but scared. Come what may, at least I'm no longer alone.

Finding Home

Jennifer Brozek is an award-winning editor and author. Winner of the 2009 Australian Shadows Award for best-edited publication, Jennifer has edited seven anthologies with more on the way. Author of *In a Gilded Light* and *The Little Finance Book That Could*, she has more than thirty-five published short stories and is an assistant editor for the award winning Apex Publications company.

Jennifer also is a freelance author for numerous RPG companies. Winner of both the Origins award and the ENnie award, her contributions to RPG sourcebooks include *Dragonlance*, *Colonial Gothic*, *Shadowrun*, *Serenity*, *Savage Worlds*, and *White Wolf SAS*.

When she is not writing her heart out, she is gallivanting around the Pacific Northwest in its wonderfully mercurial weather. Jennifer is an active member of SFWA and HWA. Read more at her blog: http://jennifer-brozek.livejournal.com/

The Wheel

By
Edward Martin III

DAY 130

    Jason looked out the window.
    "They still out there?" asked Nick.
    "I didn't know you were awake," said Jason.
    "I wake up early these days. I get nervous if I sleep too long. Is Nicole up?"
    Jason glanced toward the door to the back rooms. "I don't think so," he said. "She sleeps a lot."
    Nick sat up and stretched. His sleeping bag was half on, half off the couch. He kicked it all the way off, crouched down, and started rolling it up.
    "Y'know," said Jason. "It's okay if you just want to shove it into a corner. I don't think we've got company coming any time soon."
    "Not company we would want, anyway," muttered Nick. "I have to do this. It's…it's a normal thing. I can do this and pretend for a minute that I'm just passing through, and I stopped to visit you guys for a day or two before I take off."
    "Well, that's what you did."

"Yeah, four months ago. I think I've outstayed my invitation."

Jason shook his head. "Well, if you can find a way past that nightmare outside, you let me know. We'll both join you."

Nick tied the last loop, and stowed his bag behind the couch. He stretched again. "Yeah, right. Wouldn't that be nice? So, eggs for breakfast?"

"I thought we were out."

"Nicole found another box in the basement. Enough to make omelets for forty years."

"Who wants omelets for forty years?"

"Someone who was really into powdered eggs, man. I don't know. Wasn't he one of your buddies?"

"He was one of mine," said Nicole. She stood in the bedroom doorway, groggy. Her auburn hair stuck out all over. Dark circles shadowed under her eyes. "Well, sorta. I used to work with him. He always bragged about being able to survive the end of the world, that he had all these supplies and shit."

She shrugged. "So, when the world ended, I figured we couldn't do any worse by checking his place out."

"How'd you know where he lived?" asked Nick.

"Employee records."

"Oh, that is a total violation of HR policy, and you know it."

She flopped down into the wingback chair. That chair, the couch, and a mean little dining room table covered in cracked formica represented the bulk of usable furniture in the townhouse.

"Tell you what," she said. "When this is all over, put a note in my employee file. Until then, we eat the fuckin' eggs."

She looked over to Jason.

"They still out there?" she asked. There was no hope in her face, but she asked the question every morning. It was a ritual.

For a moment, Jason considered lying to her, and then the moment passed.

"What do you think?" he asked. "Even more, now."

Nick laced his fingers behind his head, leaned back and closed his eyes. "Well, there's no real big surprise there," he said. "Thank you very much, Leo, for going crazy last week and taking a little walk outside."

"You can't blame him," said Nicole. "It was his choice."

"Well, you're half right. Yes, it was his call to decide to go out for a walk. But it wasn't his call to go and make us this town's center of attention."

"I don't think he meant—" started Jason, but Nick cut him off.

"Don't get me wrong," he said. "I know, it's the end of the world and everything's crazy out there, and I can handle it just as well as the next guy, right. But what I don't need is someone making it just that much harder for me. None of us needs that."

They were all silent a moment, then Nick shrugged. "So, okay, there's more. Doesn't affect us, we're safe."

"For now," replied Nicole. "Supplies won't last forever."

"You mean other than powdered eggs?" asked Nick.

"I mean powdered eggs, fresh water, those cans of government food, the heating tabs, the pudding, the noodle stuff, all that shit. Eventually, it all runs out. Even the electricity, which, frankly, I'm amazed is still on. And when it all runs out, we're gonna have to go look for more, and that's when it becomes a problem—when the streets are full instead of empty."

Nick thought about it, then nodded. "Okay, yeah. That makes sense."

Day 210

Nick sat by the window, forehead pressed against the glass. "This feels very nice," he said to Jason. "Very cool on my head."

"Is it too hot in here?" asked Jason.

"Nah, I think I'm tired. I've got a headache."

"We got pills."

"Not that kind of headache."

Jason sat down on the couch, leaned back and closed his eyes. After a moment, he spoke. "You wanna play a game?" he asked.

"I'm tired of winning."

"I might win. You never know. Your headache might distract you."

Nick looked over. "I'll still win, but my headache will make me grumpy about it. I don't want to be grumpy right now. I just want my head to stop hurting."

Jason nodded. "Have you tried TV?" he asked.

"Has it worked in the past month?"

"We might find a station."

Jason rubbed his forehead against the cool glass. "Would you mind checking later?" he asked. "I'm not ready for more static."

Day 270

Nick played a card. "What's love got to do with it?" he asked.

"Got to do with it," said Nicole as she played a card.

Jason played a card. "What's love, but a secondhand emotion?"

"Who needs a heart when a heart can be broken," said Nick and played a card. "Uno."

"Uno? But, we just started," said Nicole.

"It's probably a wild card, too, isn't it?" asked Jason.

"Plus draw four," said Nick.

Jason tossed his cards on the table. "Fuck it." He stood up and walked over to the window. Stared out. "You know the nice thing about the end of the world? No more remakes." He turned to them. "Did you know they were remaking *Battlefield: Earth?* Right before this all happened."

Nick shook his head. "Jason, when you say certain words, it brings me great pain in my head. Are you being intentionally cruel?"

"I swear. I saw some shots from the production and everything."

"Bullshit," said Nicole. "That's a paradox. No way."

"What do you mean?" asked Nick.

She raised one finger. "All remakes suck worse than the original, right?"

"What about *The Thing?*" asked Jason.

"Doesn't count—it wasn't a remake. They went back to the original source material, which was a book," she replied. "So that one can't be included. All remakes of movies suck. Am I right? Am I?"

Reluctantly, they nodded.

"Hypothetically," muttered Nick.

She pointed her upraised finger at him. "Hypothetically, you can hover in the air carrying a Volvo station wagon. Doesn't mean you can. So, do they suck or not?"

He nodded. "They suck, okay."

"Good." She raised another finger. "And it's a known fact that *Battlefield: Earth* was the worst movie ever made, right."

"Right…" said Jason.

"So that means the sequel couldn't be worse, because then it wouldn't be the worst movie ever made." She beamed at them both.

Finally, Nick said, "That's not really a paradox. A paradox is a situation where things are in a causal circle, but they're all stacked up onto each other in a ring, instead of in a line. Mutually exclusive, but dependent on each other."

"Right," she said. "So, what about my movie theory? If that's not a paradox, then what is it?"

Nick sighed. "It just means that there might be a worse movie out there than *Battlefield: Earth*. Now, yes, that would suck, on an inconceivable level, but it wouldn't be a paradox."

"Besides," added Jason. "What if it wasn't a remake. What if it goes back to the original book?"

"There was a book?" asked Nicole.

"You didn't know?" asked Nick.

"I've read it twice," said Jason.

They both looked at him.

"There you are, once again, with the words that hurt my brain," muttered Nick. "Ow. Ow."

Day 304

Nick stared out the window.

Jason stepped up, looking over Nick's shoulder. "Oh hey!" he said, pointing. "Look! The end of the world!"

Slowly Nick nodded. "Yeah, but I'm still here."

"Aw, you were lucky. We were all lucky. And now we have eggs for breakfast every morning! We're living like kings, I tell you. Kings!"

"No, really," said Nick, partially to himself. "I shouldn't have been here. I was late. I was late a whole day to your place. If I'd arrived when I said I was going to arrive, I would have been on my way by the time this all happened."

Jason punched him in the shoulder. "Dude, don't even. You're fine. What—you think I'd rather you be out there? Like one of them?" He nodded his chin at the window.

Nick looked out. "I would have been wearing my bike gear," he said.

"That would have been weird. Don't do that," said Jason. "Just be here. You're fine."

Nick rolled his eyes. "You guys are fine. I'm the third wheel here."

Jason shook his head. "Just shut up," he said.

Day 368

Jason wandered out of the bedroom, yawning and stretching.

For several seconds, he stared at the empty couch, his mind a blank. Then he saw the note:

> *Jason and Nicole,*
> *Look, first of all, I won't miss the eggs.*
> *Second, you guys get more without me eating,*
> *anyway. So, that's a mixed blessing.*

I gotta go. I was on a trip anyway—and overstayed by a bit. Plus, like I said, I'm the third wheel. But I think I know what to do. I'll try to clear as much as I can away from the main streets. You guys might like a chance to get outside.

I'm going to look for people. Anyone else. But I might come back, especially if I find some really cool place that has anything other than powdered eggs. So, if you go anywhere, do me a favor and leave notes pinned to doors. I'll find you.

Cheers, mate!
Nick

Jason set the note back onto the couch, lost in thought. Then he stepped over to the window and looked out.

He looked for a long time, and finally sighed a long and satisfying sigh.

"Nicole," he called out. "Come here. Look at the street!"

He was smiling.

Edward Martin III is an award-winning filmmaker from Portland, OR. He adapted and directed an animated adaptation of H. P. Lovecraft's "The Dream-Quest of Unknown Kadath," produced *The Cosmic Horror Fun-Pak*, wrote and directed a 10-minute comprehensive period adaptation of *Lord of the Rings*, and is in deep post-production of *Flesh of my Flesh*, a ground-breaking independent zombie action movie.

He's also in development or preproduction for several other feature films, and a handful of shorts. Visit http://www.guerrilla-productions.org/ for more information.

His latest experiment is writing a horror story every week for a year. You can read the ongoing adventure at http://www.guerrilla-productions.org/Blinkspace/

Little Utopia

By
Bram E. Gieben

    The tenement building bleeds thin streams of light through cracks in boarded-up windows into the silent, abandoned street. Rob and Nancy are crouched low behind a section of wall, on the east face of the block.
    "What am I supposed to be looking at?" Rob whispers to Nancy.
    The tall, athletic perimeter guard glares at him, muscles rippling underneath her black singlet. It is August, and even at night, it is hot on the streets. "Quiet," she hisses. "Just watch."
    Rob stares hard into the darkness. There are long shadows in the escaping light of the tenement, its inhabitants eating late dinners or resting in the rooms on the top three floors of the Edwardian building. Rob is used to day-watch, and has never had very good night vision, but as he scans the street, Nancy nudges him. She points with a long, slender finger. "There."
    At the north entrance to the street their block dominates, a line of burned-out cars and scrap metal barricades the approach from the main road. In amongst the charred, twisted wrecks, Rob catches a glimpse of movement, a flicker of grey rags. His eyes

focus in, and he sees the face of the intruder: small, grubby, watchful. "I see someone," whispers Rob. Nancy silences him with a gesture.

They watch as the shivering, pale figure emerges from the tangle of wrecked cars and creeps towards the tenement's main entrance, a few feet off to the left of their position.

There are snares set by the door; large caltrops designed by the Engineers after the last incursion by a street gang from the neighbouring area. There is a heavy, mesh net concealed above the lintel, tethered to the door handle with fishing line, invisible in the darkness. The invading figure pauses by each trap and, carefully stepping through them, eventually reaches the door.

Beside Rob, Nancy tenses, ready for action. Rob puts a hand on her arm, indicating that she should wait, see if the intruder gets past the net. Nancy shakes him off.

Nancy creeps up behind the intruder, her ebony skin and black clothing making her almost invisible in the darkness. As she approaches, the ragged intruder goes suddenly still. At the last minute, the intruder whirls, turning on Nancy and aiming a roundhouse kick at her face.

Gracefully, Nancy ducks the kick, twisting her torso and sweeping back upwards with her right fist to land a hefty punch on the intruder's throat. The ragged figure goes down instantly, choking.

Nancy quickly moves in, stepping on the intruder's neck with her boot. She pulls a crossbow from the holster on her back; in a fraction of a second, she notches a razor-tipped bolt, levelling the bow at the intruder's skull.

"Wait!" Rob shouts, jumping up from his hiding place. "Stand down!" He rushes over and joins Nancy, looking down at the shivering intruder beneath the toe of her boot. "She's just a girl."

"What do you mean, 'just' a girl, Rob?" Nancy punches Rob's arm with her free hand.

"You know what I mean, don't be stupid."

The girl is no more than twenty. Her face and hands are filthy, and she looks emaciated. Anger twists her face into a leer as she struggles under Nancy's boot.

"Let me put the little mouse out of its misery," Nancy says in her cruellest voice.

"We don't know who she is," Rob says quietly. "She could be anybody. See how she picked her way through the caltrops? How quiet she was, coming through the cars? We need to talk to her, find out her story."

Nancy grunts noncommittally. She pulls her foot back and aims a swift kick at the young girl's head, knocking her unconscious. Blood blossoms from a cut on the girl's eyebrow.

Rob nods once, picks the girl up, hoists her over his shoulder, and leaves Nancy to her night vigil.

* * *

"Quiet here, isn't it?" Rob says the next morning. "A little utopia." The girl is standing on her tiptoes, peering over the wall, elbows resting on the wooden balustrade, scanning the horizon with Rob's field glasses.

"You almost wouldn't know where you were," she replies.

Rob lies on the gangplank bisecting the roof garden, eyes closed, resting, letting Sophie take in the view. An hour ago, she was brought up to the roof garden blindfolded and bound. Rob carefully removed her blindfold, untied her and introduced himself. Her name is Sarah. She seems remarkably calm, which Rob thinks could either be a bad sign, or a very good one.

"I'm sorry we had to keep you tied up last night. Nobody's sure what to do with you. Not many people pass through the city alone."

"I get it," says Sophie flatly. "You don't trust me."

"We're a small society. We only have each other to rely on. We haven't decided if we *can* trust you yet."

Rob looks down the sloping sides of the tenement roof to either side, counting the hydro tents. There is enough food growing up here to last the inhabitants of the block about six weeks, should they be unable to obtain supplies from elsewhere.

After a few minutes, Rob gestures for the field glasses.

"Where'd you get 'em?" Sophie gazes enviously at the glasses as she hands them back. "They're brilliant."

"Shaun found them for me a few months ago. He's one of our scavengers," says Rob. He passes the cracked lenses slowly across the next few streets. "Makes my job easier."

"You're a guard, then?" asks Sophie. She's still filthy from travelling the road, streaks in the grime on her face where the blindfold chafed.

Rob listens carefully to her, watching her expression for signs of fear or hostility.

"So this is what you do?" she asks him. "Watch the city; wait for trouble to come to you?"

"I'm a spotter." Rob smiles. "I'm like…the advance warning. If somebody comes, I let the others know. There are lots of different skill sets in our community. I've got good eyes, and I know the area. I grew up here. So…here I sit, most days."

He removes his canvas backpack and starts attaching a harness around his waist and legs. He chucks a similar one at Sophie. "Get yourself strapped in, let's go."

"Where to?" she asks.

"The perimeter. Back down to the street. You met our guard, Nancy, on your way in."

Sophie wrinkles her nose. "That lanky bitch who stepped on my neck and damn near killed me?"

Rob smiles, attaching a belay rope from the outer wall to his harness. "If you hadn't been alone, she probably would have killed you, and whoever you were with. You got off lightly." He attaches Sophie's harness to the rope and gives her a hand climbing onto the wall.

"You told me we were going to see the other floors," Sophie complains. "Why are we starting up here, then going all the way back down?"

"Never mind that, we'll see inside soon enough. Ever abseil before?"

Sophie fastens her ropes, puts both legs over the wall. "Aye." She laughs as she says this, as though Rob has asked a stupid question.

"On you go then." Rob watches her swing expertly out from the roof garden's walls, making her way down the side of the building with graceful efficiency.

"She could be useful," he says to himself. "Or very dangerous."

* * *

Nancy walks the block perimeter, crossbow in hand. Despite the hazy summer calm, she has a bolt pulled back against the taut cable, and her eyes restlessly scan the southeast end of the block. Back towards the north end of the street where Sophie entered the night before is the barricade made of rubbish bins, burned-out cars and scrap. Another guard, male, sits on a car bonnet there, smoking a brown roll-up, one hand dangling casually by the machete at his waist.

Rob and Sophie approach Nancy. She has the tall, lean grace of a hunter. She carefully looks Sophie up and down as the newcomer approaches.

Rob greets Nancy warmly, embracing her. The solemn woman kisses his bearded cheek. "I believe you guys have met, but let me introduce you properly. Nancy, this is Sophie. I told her you had the easy job."

"If you say so." Nancy gives one of her rare laughs, a deep, throaty chuckle. She turns to Sophie. "You were lucky last night, little mouse. If Rob hadn't been there, I'd have shot you."

Sophie blanches, but, to her credit, her voice remains steady. "Yeah. Rob keeps saying I'm lucky." She rubs the scar above her right eye. "Doesn't bloody feel like it."

"Come on now, don't get off on the wrong foot." Rob smiles, but Nancy and Sophie are eyeballing each other with grim determination. Hurriedly, he says: "Or maybe it's a bit late for that...Nancy, I'm giving Sophie here the tour of the block. She's curious about what everyone does around here. Tell her what your job is."

"I'm the muscle. If anyone gets past the perimeter, or even wants to pass by, they see me first. Usually that's enough to discourage them." She glares at Sophie. "Usually."

Giving up on defusing the tension, Rob takes Sophie by the shoulder, steering her away from Nancy towards the tower block. It is a traditional, early twentieth-century tenement; four storeys, each with one set of bay windows, interspersed with smaller rectangular ones. Many are boarded up, although the higher levels have a few open spaces, through which Rob and Sophie can see a few of the residents waking up to greet the morning.

"The bottom floor is bricked up," explains Rob, taking Sophie by the arm and leading her away from Nancy with a smile. "Nance guards the only entrance. Look up at the tenement—you see there? To the edge of the street? This is all ours. There are no un-guarded windows below the third floor. We don't take any chances."

"But who would attack you?" Sophie says. "This whole city's abandoned."

"Less abandoned than you'd think, walking through it like you did." Rob shrugs. "There are other blocks, big and small. Nice, and...not so nice."

"It isn't safe?" Sophie looks momentarily beaten.

"Safer than the streets, safer than the countryside, as long as we all play our part...Taking shifts on duty as guards, or helping tend the garden...there's lots needing done. Most of the time, I'm a spotter. I watch the horizon and the high ground to the south-east, and back, down towards the water, the docks."

"Who lives down there?"

"That's the territory of the river rats, the pirates of the Forth. You should be glad you found us before you reached the Shore."

Sophie takes in the whole street. The tenement occupied by Rob and his community is the only block in the street that isn't burned out and gutted. The graceful Edwardian tenements are empty: charred, blank windows staring like eyeless sockets.

By comparison, the ramshackle block that Rob's community occupies is well maintained. In daylight, more of the boards have been removed from the windows, and Rob watches Sophie observing the building coming to life.

On the third floor, a grey-haired man is hanging washing from a line, passing it across to another man at the next window to catch the sun. At another window, a middle-aged woman stands smoking a roll-up, eyes closed against the morning sun.

Suddenly Sophie stops, pulling up short. Her eyes are fixed on a spot beneath her feet: a series of dark, crimson-brown stains covering several slabs of pavement. Her eyes widen appreciably. "What happened here?"

"A fight. Not all intruders are as friendly as you." Rob smiles.

"What happened? Did you kill them?"

Rob says nothing.

"Did you? Tell me what happened, Rob."

Rob sighs, looks down at his feet. "The street gangs are the worst. They're just kids, mostly but…It isn't hard to take a block with a siege engine and some small arms. These bloodstains are a month or two old. They attacked with a siege tower built out of parts of a mechanical cherry picker and an old ice-cream truck…People can build anything from scrap." He looks up, meets her gaze. Rob remembers the battle; remembers caving in the skull of a small boy as he leaned in from the siege engine, hacking at the tenement with an axe. He shakes his head, trying to clear the image away from his mind's eye.

"We fought them with everything we had. Sent them packing. We must have killed half of the…people they came with. They captured three of us, though, carried them off. Three women. Marjorie, Grace and Hazel. Who knows what became of them."

Sophie swallows nervously. "Will the gang come back?"

"Almost certainly."

"But they haven't come back yet?"

"No. We put several of their heads on spikes beyond the outer wall, after the battle. That seemed to put them off. For now, at least."

Sophie blinks at Rob, her expression a mixture of fear and awe.

Rob gestures impatiently. "Come on now, we'll go and meet the others."

* * *

Sophie trails a few paces behind Rob as he makes his way up a winding stairwell lit with wan rays of sun from a grimy skylight.

On every floor, the front doors of the living areas remain open. Rob watches Sophie peer into each domicile, seeing mums cradling babies, dads preparing meals, kids playing in between the flats in raucous, laughing tumbles.

"People raise kids here?" asks Sophie.

"Those that survive. The winters are cold, and we have barely any access to medicine."

"How many people are there in the block?"

"Near three hundred at the last count. Everyone knows everyone." Rob turns back to meet Sophie's eyes. "No kids where you come from?"

She pauses before she answers. "Not much of anything where I come from."

Rob waits for more, but Sophie stays quiet. He leads her inside one of the flats. The walls have been knocked through to make one big room, which is a mass of tubing, wiring, metal, piles of wood, saws and hammers and other tools. Scrap covers every available surface, piled up in great drifts on dilapidated desks, leaning in great hulking piles in every corner. In and around this rusting mess, adults and children move nimbly and efficiently, searching through the detritus as easily as if it were an alphabetical list.

One blond girl notices the new arrivals, and comes to greet them. Her cheeks are dotted with freckles, her overalls with oil. She sticks out a grimy hand. "Hello, Rob. Who's your girlfriend?"

Rob winces. "Fiona MacHuill, meet Sophie Connell." Sophie shakes the young girl's hand; her grip is firm. "All the people in this flat are MacHuills or their partners; give or take a few."

"What do you do?" Sophie asks Fiona.

"My Dad was a plumber and joiner, before the troubles. Taught us everything before he passed on. We keep the water running, fix broken stuff. That's how it is here. We all work, each according to their particular skills."

Sophie says nothing, just nods, her eyes taking in the crowded, bustling room. As she turns away, a glance passes between Rob and Fiona, full of meaning.

Fiona leans in close and whispers to Rob. "I don't trust her. She looks shifty."

"We didn't trust you at first," Rob whispers back. "Then look what happened."

Fiona elbows him sharply in the ribs. "She's a stranger Rob. Just think for once, alright? And **not** with your dick." She turns away, striding quickly into the chaos of the room.

* * *

As they ascend to the third floor, Rob introduces Sophie to Tom Templesmith, who tends the roof garden. He too is friendly, but as Tom gives her the same appraising, noncommittal look up and down that Fiona MacHuill did, Sophie begins to look nervous. Rob says nothing.

On the fourth floor, a family called the Bedfords are making grain alcohol. Rob holds up a jar of colourless liquid. "It'll take the back of your head off if you're not careful, but it passes the time."

Sophie gratefully accepts a small sip, and then a bigger glug. "Not bad," she says, coughing.

On the top floor are a group of mechanics and plumbers. "They're not a family," explains Rob, "More like a tribe. The Engineers, we call them."

The Engineers all defer to Kathleen, a redheaded Irish woman. Sophie asks lots of questions about Kathleen's job, her workers, what materials are used and what they build. Rob nods approval; the two women seem to like each other. After a while, Kathleen beckons one of her 'tribe' over, a balding man in a leather apron. She sends Rob away with her assistant.

"Show Rob the dynamo project, Kinsey." Her accent is a soft, Dublin lilt, almost melodic.

Rob raises his eyebrows, walks away, chatting amiably with Kinsey. Kathleen turns to face Sophie. She is a handsome woman, tall and broad-shouldered.

"I haven't got long," she says. "Rob will be back in a minute. It's just…Look, you seem alright. And I know how you feel, OK? I was an outsider when I arrived. We're a small society, far from perfect."

Sophie nods. "Rob calls it a utopia."

"He's leaving out the bad stuff. Rob's an idealist. He sees the best in people."

"I knew it," Sophie sighs. "Too good to be true. What is it? You're cannibals, aren't you?"

Kathleen laughs. "Cannibals! Not likely. Don't get me wrong, Sophie. Life's hard here on the block. Precarious. If a gang wants in, all they need are superior numbers and firepower. If the government came with troops, we'd have to defend ourselves. We lose too many to illnesses, to violence." Kathleen places a hand on Sophie's arm. "You just…you seem like a nice person. Smart, helpful. When Rob asks you if you want to stay, just think about that, alright? We need folk like you."

Sophie smiles politely, but says nothing.

Returning, Rob bids the Engineers and their boss goodbye, then leads Sophie back out to the hallway.

At the top of the tenement, Rob uses a pole to hook down the stepladder up to the roof access, and gestures Sophie to go on up ahead of him.

Chewing her lip, she climbs the ladder.

* * *

Up on the roof, dusk is falling. The sky is a hazy, burnt orange. Rob and Sophie sit opposite each other on the gangplank, smoking a joint.

"What do you think of our little utopia, then?" Rob asks.

"You keep calling it that. It isn't perfect, Rob," says Sophie. "Neither am I…But I think I could be useful to you."

"Are you asking if you can stay?" He stubs out the roach, meeting her eyes.

"Are you asking me to?" she replies.

Rob steeples his hands. "If we let you stay, and you let us down, or betray us, we could live to regret it. We have to be careful. You've seen everything now. You know names, faces. You could run to another block, to the gangs, or the pirates, and tell them our weaknesses."

"I wouldn't do that!" Sophie quickly scrambles for a response, but Rob cuts her off.

"You don't seem the type. I think you're on the level—you want to be part of a community, to be safe. I think you understand that nobody here gets a free ride." Rob frowns. "But you could just be a good liar. We haven't paid taxes here since the troubles, you know."

Sophie looks crestfallen. "You think I'm from the government?"

"They've sent envoys before," Rob says. "We've had to…deal with them. But first, we offered them a choice, just like we're offering you."

"If I was a spy, why would I be alone? And bloody starving to boot? You saw the state of me when I arrived last night."

Rob smiles. "You made it through our traps pretty efficiently, though. Like you knew where they would be. I can't help but wonder about that. Let's say you are a spy. I have no way of knowing how deep your cover is. That's why we're up here, Sophie. You need to convince me. I need to be sure."

"And what about you lot? You kill people! It's all well and good calling them gangs, or pirates, or whatever…you killed people, Rob."

"We did what we had to." Rob breaks her gaze, looks off into the evening sky. "We became what we had to be…to survive."

"Besides, you think the government even cares about a small settlement like this? They've got whole cities to take back." Sophie pauses. "That's what I heard."

"You might be right," admits Rob. "Myself, I don't think they'll come. They told us to take care of ourselves: that's what we do. There's no safety net anymore. We understand." Rob takes a deep breath. "But I hear they've been recruiting mercenaries from Neo France and the Belgian Republic. Real hard bastards, who fought in Singapore and Cataluña. 'Contractors,' they're calling them. Mercenaries, more like. They want the cities back."

"I'm no mercenary, look at me!" Sophie exclaims.

"You've heard of them, though. And as you proved last night, you're pretty handy at sneaking about. Not to mention that roundhouse kick you tried on Nancy. She's hard as nails, and quick as lightning, so she ducked it. If it had been another guard, if it had been me? I think you'd have got through our perimeter. That worries me, Sophie. So…convince me," says Rob. "Give me a reason to trust you, to trust your story."

Sophie sighs. "I'm not sure I can."

"It's OK. Take your time," says Rob. "I'm patient." He reaches under the flap of the nearest hydro tent and plucks a fresh carrot from the soil, cleaning off the dirt. He takes a bite and hands it to Sophie. "This is delicious, try it."

She bites, chews.

"How did you make it here alone, Sophie? I need to know."

Her answer is just a little too quick. "I've travelled alone since the troubles. I just like it that way."

Rob shifts position. "A clever person like you, all by yourself, travelling city to city. Sorry, I don't buy it. You wouldn't have survived."

Sophie shrugs. "Guess I'm just lucky."

"Lucky, aye. Or perhaps you were dropped into the city by military drone. Perhaps you aren't alone after all—maybe your unit is around the corner, out of sight, waiting to overrun my block." Rob smiles, trying to be nice. "I have to consider that."

Sophie moves closer now, bathed in the fading light, smiling in a kittenish way. "Lucky, lucky, lucky…Maybe you could be lucky too, Rob." She leans over, kisses him. Then she places his hand on her neck, letting it slide down to the first button of her blouse. Under her clothing, her skin is clean.

Afterwards, Rob pretends to sleep as she steals down the stairs. He watches her evade the perimeter guards, sneaking nimbly through shadows. She is fast, graceful, careful.

Dangerous.

"No one's perfect," he breathes.

He flicks a pebble down to land near Nancy, signalling her to give chase.

There is a pause, and then he hears the click-clack of a crossbow bolt being pulled back.

Finding Home

Bram E. Gieben grew up in Edinburgh, where 'Little Utopia' is set. He is currently undertaking the MLitt in Creative Writing at the University of Glasgow. As a writer, he wears his influences on his sleeve—a habit he hopes to rid himself of, one day.

    A veteran of the Scottish Slam Poetry scene, Bram is a member of literary performance collectives Writers' Bloc and the Chemical Poets. In 2010, he co-wrote and performed the live show 'Twenty Tentacle' at the Edinburgh Fringe, and in 2011 he wrote and starred in his own show, 'Neuromonster.' He has competed in poetry slams across the UK and the world, everywhere from Auckland, to Bristol, to New York City.

    In 2007, Bram set up fiction website Weaponizer.co.uk, an open-source project for emerging writers of SF, horror and other alternative short fiction. The site publishes the work of over eighty writers worldwide, and recently launched a quarterly magazine.

    Bram also makes music under the name Texture, helping to run the Black Lantern Music netlabel. Since 2005, he has written regularly for the Scottish music press, helping to set up the successful free paper *The Skinny*. His fiction has been published on BoingBoing and 6 Sentences, and in *Drey Quarterly*.

http://texturemusick.tumblr.com

Gaia's Legacy

By
David Kernot

The Earth shook.

Alan pulled himself from his small bunk and raced outside into a new dawn. By the time he stood on the launch pad next to the scramjet, *Andromeda*, the ground had stopped shaking. Tsunami was his first thought; they were vulnerable this close to the shore. Out across the Equatorial Sea, poisonous brown scum floated on the choppy surface, a constant reminder of the world's failure.

He ran down onto Europa Base's beach, past the dinghy, but everything looked the same: half-dead palm trees, and the tall, buckled structures of the space launch site. He wiped his brow. Had nobody else heard it? He needed to wake Lisa, in case there was trouble. He strode back toward the small ring of huts that formed the scientific camp's sleeping quarters.

"Dr. Derringer!"

Alan stopped. He turned to face one of their security team. "Did you feel that?"

"Yes. The national seismic center confirmed it was a size 3.8 tremor, about 50 klicks behind us into the hills."

"No tsunami threat then?"

"No, but strangely enough about thirty quakes hit at the same time all across the Earth."

"Thirty?"

"Yep, and there are no reports of damage anywhere. It's like someone drove a great rumbling truck across the world and then vanished."

Alan nodded. It had sounded like a truck rumbling along. "Bizarre. I suppose I'll find out more soon enough. I'll be back at Meridian City today. I'll go and check out the *Andromeda*, just to be sure." The lie came easily enough; truth was he dreaded climbing aboard. "No issues last night?" asked Alan.

"No, but trouble comes in waves. I suspect your launch today will bring the apocos back, that or the quake."

Alan frowned. "Apocos? Apocalypse survivors?"

The guard nodded.

"So, how dangerous is it here?"

"They're not that much trouble; they come for the tech mainly, food, or anything else they can get their hands on."

"Are there really as many as the reports say?"

"There are about twelve hundred survivors. They live in a cave about 20 klicks up the coast."

Alan thought about it. "That's a lot of people. Sure they won't try to invade?"

The guard shrugged.

Alan laughed. The man was a veteran. "I take it you're staying then, Master Sergeant?"

"You bet."

Alan stepped onto the launch pad uneasily, and walked around the scramjet, checking *Andromeda's* panels and external structure. He stopped at the highly polished golden plaque covered in engraved symbols; the Earth in relation to the Sun, Earth's place in the universe, and a naked man and woman. It was standard fare for all spacecraft since the 1970's Voyager Space Probes. *Andromeda* should have tasted the cold of deep space, with him as pilot. But they ended up serving in different ways: Alan as microbiologist, and *Andromeda* as cargo vessel.

"Do you miss it, Dr. Derringer?"

Alan turned. He had forgotten the guard. "Miss it?"

"Space travel. Weren't you *Andromeda*'s pilot?"

Alan nodded. "Long time ago."

"Ever want captain her again?"

Alan took a deep breath. "Sometimes." The word tasted false. All the time would have been too much of an admission, especially if he could have changed what had happened. "For the most part, I'm happy to let the AI autopilots do their job." He thought about *Andromeda*'s sister ship, *Centaurus*, long since destroyed, and sighed. He looked down at his shaking hands and realized it might as well have been yesterday. At least *Andromeda*, had survived. "At least we don't get the same human errors."

"So an AI would have saved the crew's lives?" The guard knew his history, and why wouldn't he?

Alan shrugged. His chest tightened and his voice caught with emotion. "Perhaps, I don't know. Sometimes we think we're unbreakable. Age teaches you otherwise." He looked up at the blackened ruins nearby. "This was to be our push to Mars, and then it all stopped."

"But they came to us."

"The signal from the Drake Outpost?" It was true the listening station on the dark side of the moon heard *something*; an abnormal alpha transmission, but alien life?

"Yes, sir. They found us."

Alan took a deep breath, and breathed easier. "I think we may have found them. Perhaps because they noticed one of our probes, or heard all our EM radiation and noise."

"So they're coming to shut us up?"

Alan laughed. "Perhaps. That's what the guys on the Drake Outpost will discover. Turn your TVs down, there's too many reruns of *Leave it to Beaver* and *I Love Lucy* propagating across the universe."

"You're funny, Dr. Derringer."

"Call me Alan."

"I don't know if I could, sir, but I'm Geoff. We'll see each other again, I've got eight months before I get down to Mawson City."

Alan thought about the stray shots, and the missing scientific gear and decided that Geoff was a typical soldier and loved his job. "So what's it like at Mawson City?"

"It's nice. All that land and fresh water, plus there's the shrinking ice pack in the center. I've heard it's better than your continent. What do they call it? The dry ring colony? Miserably cold North Pole Sea one minute, frozen ice the next. Give me the South Pole any day."

Alan laughed over the world's choices. He'd been a teenager twenty years ago, when twenty billion people tried to crowd the poles. "Better than here. What is it at the equator now a mild 115 degrees? But you might be right. I might take Leece down to Mawson City one day. Never been down to Antarctica."

"So when are you and Dr. Moran going to tie the knot?"

"Leece and I?" That surprised him. They weren't even dating. "She's my research assistant."

"If you say so."

Alan smiled. "Are my feelings that obvious?"

The guard nodded. "It's written all over her face too. Marry her."

He chuckled. "That's good to know, but we're not dating."

The guard leaned back and frowned. "Why in heavens not?"

Alan shrugged. "We're always together as it is. I think there's an understanding between us, but it never seems to be the right time to talk about it."

"Don't let her get away."

"I don't intend to." Alan reached up and unlatched a small panel on the scramjet and pressed a button. A large door panel pushed out from the craft's smooth surface. He unhooked it, and then stepped back as it lowered to become a ramp. Alan forced a smile and pushed back his discomfort at climbing inside *Andromeda*. "I'll go in and check the systems."

"Don't want to play second fiddle with the AI?"

"Something like that."

"Sit your girl up in the flight cabin, I hear the view is awesome. Pop the question then."

Alan felt for the ring box in his pocket. "About living together, sure. As to the rest, you never know."

"I'll come back and see you both off."

Alan nodded and stepped inside. He went over the checks again and again, like he had before they left Meridian City. He couldn't afford a repeat of *Centaurus.* Leece would be on the flight. He broke into a cold sweat thinking about her lovely skin burning like parchment…no, he couldn't think about that.

* * *

As Lisa stepped from the research hut, Alan realized that as much as he hated this place, the lack of people was a blessing.

"It's not too bad here," she said, sinking her toes into the sand. "At least, it won't be when when your oxygen producing bacteria clean up these poisoned oceans. What are you going to call your new find?"

"I thought I could name it after you."

She laughed mischievously. "We *could* stay, and I'll work on that all-over tan for you."

He laughed back. "I've calculated that at the rate the bacteria are multiplying, the sea could be back in balance within three to five years. It might be possible to rebuild a decent colony in the equatorial region."

"We could wait it out here," she said.

"Sitting and watching you get an all over tan would make an interesting study." A warm glow lit his cheeks.

"Last chance, mister? Bikini top goes away until our next visit."

She had that look that Alan loved.

"Sadly, as romantic as a hut by the sea is, I suspect I will have to report to Bill in Meridian as soon as possible."

"Later then?"

"Absolutely. The bacteria will need monitoring."

Finding Home

The scramjet's engines started up the beach.

"Let's go then," said Alan.

"Did you send the report to Bill?"

"Err, yes." He knew Bill wouldn't be happy to report their findings. "He will be hopping mad when he reads it. I said the tests failed, and I switched the results."

"What? Serious? We are going to keep the results from the northern government?"

"Yes, and the southern government. I'm taking samples to Meridian. We'll classify it so they won't have access to the data. Nobody outside the team needs to know while the bloom here is healthy and continues to grow. Until we can be sure there won't be any negative effects from spawning the bacteria elsewhere."

He gave Lisa's hand a squeeze as they walked towards the jet. She squeezed back. He wondered if he should ask her to marry him on the trip back home. Perhaps at the New Year's celebrations.

Geoff, the Master Sergeant, was waiting at the scramjet. He saluted and then grinned at Alan.

"There's still a couple of chairs in the front for you, Captain, if you needed a better view." The guard winked.

Alan nodded, and his cheeks burned. But as he stepped inside, uneasiness returned.

Alan's cheeks were cool by the time he locked the door and sat, but his nervousness had escalated.

Leece leaned in when they were seated. "Captain? What was that all about?"

He forced a smile. Inside *Andromeda*, it didn't seem funny, and his palms went sweaty. He rubbed them on his jumper. "I'll tell you...maybe once we're stable, after launch."

"You don't like flying do you?"

He shook his head.

"You know it's the safest form of transport," she said and squeezed his hand. "Don't worry, I'll keep your mind off things." She giggled.

He closed his eyes and nodded. It would be harder than she could imagine.

* * *

Memories unfolded from a lifetime ago…

On the launch pad at Europa Base, he felt *Centaurus'* vibrations inside *Andromeda*. His radio squawked…

Captain Melanie Grayson said, "Good luck, *Andromeda*."

Alan barely contained his excitement, "Back at you, *Centaurus*."

"See you on the dark side of the moon."

Base Command: "*Centaurus* launched."

"God speed, *Centaurus*." Alan's voice was barely a whisper.

Seconds later, he felt *Andromeda's* lift, and braced himself for the culmination of his dreams.

Base Command: "Problem with *Centaurus*—"

Base Command: "Aborting mission…*Andromeda*, brace, brace…"

Alan tensed. *Centaurus'* impact wrenched Alan from his seat, sent him across the cockpit into the far wall. He remembered his arm snapping, his shoulder dislocating…

Everything went blank.

* * *

"Alan, we're here."

Lisa shook him and slowly, he forced himself upright.

"Alan, wake up, this is the best part, the view of Meridian."

"Okay, awake." He rubbed his eyes and looked out the scramjet's projected window image. His hand went to his shoulder, feeling the scar tissue and the pin. He took a breath and pushed away the memories of *Centaurus* and his fiancée, Captain Melanie Grayson. The tall domes of the polar ringed city sparkled, stood proud amongst the frozen tundra.

Alan only wished that there were more accommodating places to live. High world temperatures, oil-contaminated water, desalination plant toxic salt waste, a slough of poisoned, radiated lands from power plants, all spread across the oceans. The Poles, with their fresh, untapped water, and most tolerable temperatures, were all the globe had left to offer. Unless the bacteria could change that.

Tonight, he decided. He smiled. "Come with me to New Year's in Meridian Square?"

"Really?"

"Yes, something I want to tell you."

"Ooh, mysterious. Tell me now." She grinned.

He grinned back at her and the muscles in his cheeks tightened. "Something I want to *ask* you then."

"Oh, sounds *very* important," she said, mimicking his serious tone.

Alan smiled. She *had* to know, everything about her screamed she knew. He took a deep breath. "Tonight, then?"

"I wouldn't miss it."

He took a breath.

The scramjet shook.

"That's strange," said Lisa, sitting up straighter. "Did you feel that?"

"I did." He leaned forward and looked at the window display.

"Shuttle 141, move to holding pattern," barked a metallic voice from the front speaker. "We have a problem with the landing pad."

Alan looked out. A crack opened up in the tarmac, growing wider and wider. White condensed steam puffed out. "Leece." A building shook and then collapsed. The cracks widened and the building vanished.

Gaseous fire belched from the ice near the landing pad, and a rift opened in the permafrost. Lava spewed into the air. He punched an override code into the keypad on his armrest, and spoke into a recessed microphone. "Initiate climb to 5000 feet!" The jet rose, shaking as it travelled through pockets of hot air.

"How did you do that?"

"They gave me access," he said.

Alan looked below. Dozens of vents opened up around Northern Alliance cities. The lava spread. In minutes, it covered the settlement. Buildings collapsed. Some leaned and then fell into the pool of grey-red molten lava. Steam bloomed from the icy sea when it quenched the flowing lava. He grabbed the phone from the seat console and dialed Bill.

"Bill, what the hell's happening?"

"I'm at home…with the family…everything around me is shaking," yelled Bill.

"Can you take cover?"

"I don't know? It's my girl's fourth birthday tomorrow—she's with us now—and all the cakes and candy bags are shaking. I don't know how it will go, if this all—"

The phone went dead. "Bill?"

More silence followed.

"Bill?"

Below him, the city erupted in a flash of red lava. Like a river it spread, covered Meridian and swept everything up in its path. Everything vanished in a few blinks of the eye. He felt numb, lost for words.

Bill and his family; three daughters were down there, the rest of the team too. All his friends; everybody he had ever known. Cold clawed within him. He couldn't fathom what had just happened, and he shook his head. It was indescribable, simply beyond comprehension. How could an entire population vanish? He felt ill and wanted to vomit, but as he bent over and stared at his shoes, nothing came except tears.

He wanted to say something, but words wouldn't form. Lisa sat rigid, staring at the window image, hands over her mouth, screaming into the silence.

He touched the intercom, pressed some arm-pad keys. "Climb and fly to Mawson City?"

Leece turned to him and croaked. "The South Pole? We can't leave."

He understood her logic. Stay, look for survivors, do something. "There's nothing we can do here, Leece. There's nobody left."

Finding Home

She nodded, and closed her eyes on tears.

Alan took a deep breath and exhaled slowly. The scramjet's shaking added to his uneasiness. He unclipped his seat belt, stood up, and placed his hand on her shoulder. "There are people down in the south, trauma therapists…it won't be long until—"

The craft shook and he gripped the chair. Geeze! He leaned into Leece, "I'm going to sit up front with the AI. Coming?" He held out his hand and waited.

The craft lurched sideways and Alan sailed across the cabin. He hit the cabin wall and tumbled to the floor. Everything went black. When he opened his eyes, the floor carpet was inches from his nose. Disorientated, he looked around the cabin. Everything spun. He closed his eyes, aware of the shooting pain in his neck that continued down his left arm. He tried to sit up, but his arm wouldn't obey. It left a bitter taste in his mouth. The pin had broken away, sliced through his nerves; just what he'd been told would happen if he didn't take care. Yet another reason to retire. *Andromeda* was cursed, and now his arm was paralyzed.

The scramjet continued to shake. It lurched left and then right.

Leece appeared next to him. "Are you alright?"

He focused, tried to still the spinning, and nodded. The scramjet's flight path didn't seem right.

"Help me up. I need to get to the flight cabin." Autopilot could be ineffective. Hot pockets of air were playing havoc with the AI. It wasn't human. It didn't comprehend.

He raised his right arm. Leece helped him up and into the empty flight deck. He strapped himself into the pilot's chair and took the controls.

He had been too long away from the pilot's seat. Leece took the seat beside him and strapped herself in. "What are you going to do?"

"The AI can't cope. We're going to have to do it ourselves."

"Fly it?" Her hands went to her mouth. "When did you become a pilot?"

"Technically, I didn't. I'm an ex-astronaut…deep-space trained. This was my ship, *Andromeda*, before they did the mods for Earth flights. I know everything about her." He touched the instrumentation panel.

"You've never mentioned this before?"

He closed his eyes and swallowed. When he opened them again, his voice caught. "I don't like talking about my failures. If she wasn't sound, I reckon we'd have found out already." He leaned in and looked at her. "We don't want that, do we?"

"No." She shook her head. Color seeped back into her face.

He looked at the projected images—their 'window' outside—down at the chaotic sea of molten lava below. How could so much of the Earth be covered? Volcanic ash reduced their visibility and he wondered how long it would be before the cameras were ruined by ash. His eyes danced over the gauges. Everything looked good.

His left arm hung lifeless as he took a breath. He disengaged the AI. Using his right hand, he pulled back on the controls and felt her climb out of the jets of lava. The South Pole wouldn't be hard to find, and he could switch on the AI when they arrived. He wasn't ready to attempt a landing.

* * *

Alan hoped that the knot in his stomach would relinquish its grip as the South Pole and Mawson City loomed closer. But molten lava covered the land. Nothing remained and there was no sign of standing buildings or life.

"How? Why?" said Leece.

He shook his head. "I have no idea…"

"Where do we go now?"

Looking at the sea of molten lava, Alan was beyond words. The Poles had been humanity's last stand.

"Why?"

Again he had no answer. The knot in his stomach tightened to match the lump in his throat.

"What now?" Leece's tears fell unhindered.

"There's the Drake Outpost—" he forced out.

"The moon?"

He nodded. "As a last resort, but I don't think I'm capable of flying *Andromeda* there. There has to be somewhere else—"

"What about Europa Base?"

"Of course." He nodded. Why didn't he think of that? He squeezed her hand. "We can only hope."

Alan adjusted *Andromeda's* flight path and pushed the old girl up and away from the crippling images of what had been Mawson City. Leece sat next to him, but she was moving into shock. He needed to talk to her, keep her mind on other things, but what could he say? He couldn't think of anything, and he had to keep the scramjet up and out of the hot jets of air and lava. Above, a blanket of thick ash closed in.

He had no idea what to do if Europa wasn't there. They climbed into sub-orbital space for a horrific view of a world on fire. As they flew into the night, a sea of molten red glowed angrily below them, but it grew cold in the cabin. He grabbed a blanket and put it over Leece's shoulders, but she didn't register or shift her glazed stare.

* * *

At the Equator, Alan sat up and felt his first glimmer of relief. "Well I'll be darned. Leece, take a look." He switched the AI back on and set it to land.

She turned to him. "How?"

"I don't know." His neck ached, and his arm still wouldn't respond, but the knot in his stomach loosened. He had no idea how the sea and this part of the world had been left untouched by volcanic activity.

As they stepped out of the scramjet, Alan was shocked to find everything exactly as they had left it.

"Where are the guards?" asked Leece when nobody met them.

"I don't know."

"So what do we do now?"

"For the moment, take stock of rations and equipment. I'm going to spend the afternoon stripping *Andromeda*. Then I reckon we should get some rest."

"So we're not flying to the moon?"

He shook his head and looked at the scramjet. "I wouldn't trust her to remain airtight in space."

* * *

Alan woke at the banging on the door of the hut and man's voice calling out. "Dr. Derringer." It was ten in the morning, and he smiled at Leece, next to him in the bed.

She smiled back. "You should answer that. I think our honeymoon is over." She raised her left hand and stared at the ring.

"Just a minute," he yelled through the door.

"Roger that."

As nice as their night had been, it had been a wild, passionate moment, where they had pushed reality away for a few hours, for a night. Together, they stepped out into a sun-filled vista. Here, what had happened yesterday at Meridian and Mawson City seemed remote.

Alan was surprised to see a dozen or so poorly dressed men and women with Geoff. They looked back at Alan with suspicion.

Geoff stepped forward, away from the group. "Dr. Moran." He smiled at Leece, gesturing to the sling. "Have an accident, Dr. Derringer?"

"Yes, during the flight out of Meridian City." Alan's voice caught in his throat.

"Is it true? You saw it for yourself?"

Alan closed his eyes. Emotion welled up inside of him. He felt Leece grab his hand and squeeze it tight. He took a deep breath, barely able to speak. "Yes, both cities were completely destroyed. I'm sorry."

Through a firestorm of emotions, the man was still able to say, "How?"

Alan shook his head. He had nothing to add.

"So, we're all that's left?"

"It is possible there are pockets of people," said Alan, indicating the group behind Geoff.

Geoff cleared his throat. "Yep, these are good people. When we heard the news of what was happening, we went to see about getting their help. We gave them our medical supplies, and they've promised to speak to their leaders and their military for us. We should be safe enough, but I admit it is a bit risky."

"So you're going to join them?"

"Yep. They're living in a cave by the sea. The water and conditions are far better than we had believed."

"Better how?"

Geoff shrugged. "Come with us, sir, and find out. I'm sure that with your expertise you'll be welcomed."

Alan looked at Leece. "Well?"

She nodded. "I want to discover why this region has been unaffected by the chaos."

Geoff stepped forward. "Perhaps it's the bacteria?" Alan frowned. "I don't see how. Bacteria don't quell volcanic activity."

"Perhaps Mother Earth, Gaia, is telling us something?"

"No, the scientist in me can't buy that either."

"What then?"

Alan sighed. "Honestly, I have no idea."

"Then stay here, sir, take more measurements, find out what's going on. Research the bacteria and this region."

Leece stepped forward and put her hand on his arm. "What alternatives do we have, Alan?"

Alan turned and looked at *Andromeda*.

"You should launch her into space, sir, as a tribute to the fallen," said Geoff. "God knows what we are going to do with her otherwise."

Emotion churned within him and the memories of *Centaurus* and her launch grew. What use was *Andromeda* now to anyone here?

"What about it, Dr. Derringer?"

Alan looked at them, aware that all eyes were on him.

* * *

The trip to the settlement was more than a journey. For Alan and Leece it was the start of a new life, and they had no doubts as to the coming hardships.

It had felt right to launch *Andromeda*, to allow her to begin her journey into deep space. It was a fitting tribute to the people of Mawson City and of Meridian City, who had perished, and to the crew of *Centaurus*.

Pulling out the mission data from *Andromeda's* navigation computer, and punching in the same mission coordinates as the original Cassini Probe had been an act of blind faith; to send her out into the far reaches of the universe for another civilization.

He had to believe that there was some truth to the signals received by the Drake Outpost on the moon; but they'd never really know. Putting the bacteria samples aboard felt right, too, a gift to the cosmos. Perhaps *Andromeda* would find other life.

No matter what else happened to Earth, the bacteria tucked away in *Andromeda's* hold could one day become Gaia's legacy.

David Kernot is an Australian science fiction, fantasy and horror writer. His writing credits include *AlienSkin Magazine*, *AntipodeanSF*, *Flashes in the Dark*, and *MicroHorror*. Up and coming work will appear in *Aoife's Kiss*, *Black House Comics*, *Darwin's Evolutions*, and *Midnight Echo*. He is a member of the Online Writing Workshop, and member and editor of the Andromeda Spaceways Inflight Magazine co-operative. He was also Contributing Editor for *Midnight Echo Issue 6*.

David spends his days hiding behind a large Mountain Ash desk, surrounded by pictures of the Flinders Ranges, editing his yet unpublished Kingdom of Isalde fantasy series, and an urban horror, Seventeen Souls. More information can be found at www.davidkernot.com

Part II:
The Periphery

Unicorn Chaser

By
Minerva Zimmerman

Captain's Log 8-27-57 1100:
Spent last evening indulging pollywogs and scouts with stories of 24-hour taco stands, grocery stores, 7-11 Slurpees and cartoon marathons. Sometimes I wish I'd paid a little closer attention to world events and less time on obscure animes about catboys. It makes questions like, "What did you do in the Before Times?" a little awkward sometimes.

Saw a six-legged unicorn. First new mutation I've seen in a long time. Maybe the little monsters are getting more genetically stable. I guess genetically engineered creatures have always been more prone to mutation, and the kitten-sized Tarlow unicorns especially so.

I shouldn't hope that they'll stop mutating. Eventually they'll even be able to eat the eucalyptus and succulents that provide what greenery we've got left. There's not much left of—

Finding Home

"Moooooooom! Spike won't let me feed the fish."

I set down my pen and waited for Phin to thunder up the stairs to what used to be a projection booth and now functioned as my office and bedroom.

"What happened the last time you were sent to feed the fish?" I asked.

"That wasn't my fault," whined Phin. "Dash dumped it all in one tank. Not me."

"Whose job was it to feed the fish? Yours or Dash's?" *Lord, grant me strength and patience to let him see his ninth birthday.*

"But he did it!"

I sighed and tried to keep my voice level and patient. "It doesn't matter who did it. It was your responsibility and fish died. You've lost my trust and the trust of the station. You need to work hard to regain your rank."

"That's not fair." Phin stamped his foot against the threadbare movie theater carpet.

"You just earned yourself a week grinding unicorn chitin."

He opened his mouth to argue.

"Do I need to make it two?"

"No, Captain." Phin glared at me and stomped his way back out of the theater muttering, "CJ wouldn't make me do baby chores."

"Your brother has enough to worry about," I said futilely as the theater doors swung wildly in Phin's wake.

A headache blossomed between my eyes.

After the winter floods, CJ had recruited a group of twenty-three, mostly teenagers or young adults, and left to form their own station at Fashion Valley. The group felt they should be promoted to higher ranks. Given the number of higher-ranking elders unlikely to croak soon enough, and murder still a socially unacceptable hobby even after the apocalypse...

I think CJ expected me to stop them. He seemed surprised when I gave them two months of food and assistance setting up their own hydroponics and fish tanks.

Of the original twenty-three, two returned here to Mission Valley and two more joined Hazard Center when they discovered adapting the empty shell of a mall to living areas and food production was harder than maintaining existing ones.

I thought they'd all return within a few months, but CJ had my stubbornness and the station persevered for going on six months now. Fashion Valley was in rough shape because of the decades of yearly flood damage, but they've reclaimed the entire northeast corner.

* * *

I rubbed at the skin between my eyes, trying to soothe away the Phin-induced headache.

The walkie-talkie behind me crackled to life, "Captain?" I almost knocked the handset to the ground in my haste to grab it. "Kara here, go ahead."

"There's been a break-in," said Alonzo's voice.

I looked at the channel the message had come in on. Seventeen, good—not a public frequency. "Where?"

"Someone pried open the backdoor to CPK. Didn't take much, some tools, lights and protein cakes, but the door's bent. Can't get it closed."

Damnit. That meant unicorns in food storage. "How bad?"

"Maybe a few dozen?"

Overnight, a few dozen unicorns could turn into a few hundred. "Do what you can," I said. "I'm on my way."

I changed to general frequency on the walkie-talkie. "Are May and Leaf back?"

"Negative," came Wolfwood's reply.

"What's your twenty, Wolf?" I asked my middle son and grabbed a unicorn spear.

"Lobby."

Wolf and his twin sister, Kitara, lounged in the cool of the lobby. Wolf looked at the spear in my hand and grabbed one for himself and another for Kit. "Trouble?"

He'd never been much of a talker. Solid as a rock and rolled with anything life threw at him with grace and acceptance. Just like his father.

I bit my cheek to keep from getting choked up. *I miss that man.* "Break-in at CPK," I said. "Door's busted and there's unicorns inside."

Mothers don't have favorite children, but their father had been my favorite partner. I patted Wolf's shoulder instead of the hug I desperately wanted. At sixteen, he shuns random hugs.

Outside, the air hummed with foraging dragonflies from the nearby San Diego River. Nearer than it used to be, but still far enough away that it didn't flood the mall in the winter like at Fashion Valley. Flooding was the main reason there'd never been a long-term station established at Fashion. Several groups had tried, but it'd always been abandoned. I sighed. *Was likely to be abandoned again.*

"We're going to need to seal the door," I said.

"I'll get the shrink wrap kit." said Kit and headed off.

Wolf slung a containment bag over his shoulder and sighed.

"What?" I asked.

"CJ's an idiot."

"Don't talk about your brother that way," I said, but couldn't put much weight behind the words. "He'll learn."

"Or people die," said Wolf.

He might be six years younger, but Wolf had twice the sense of his elder brother.

"I won't let that happen." I managed to sound confident even if I didn't fully believe it.

* * *

The damage was worse than Alonzo led me to believe. The thieves pried the door open on the hinge side, breaking one and ripping the metal of the door. It needed welding and a lot of banging to get it closed again.

This was the work of someone who didn't care who they hurt. Callous indifference or true desperation? None of the other stations were in bad straits that I knew of. None were even struggling except for CJ's Fashion Valley—but even they weren't, shouldn't be, desperate. If things were that bad, CJ would ask for assistance—wouldn't he?

"Damnit," I muttered under my breath. Then louder, "As soon as the door is shrink-wrapped, take it off."

The two young women standing guard nodded. One of them speared a tiny unicorn before it could wedge through the opening into the storehouse.

Laughing ensigns from Fashion Valley attracted our attention down the trolley tracks to the west as they goofed off, enjoying their festival furlough. I watched my guards' eyes harden and mouths twist in anger. It didn't matter if the young men were guilty of the crime; my people believed they might be. *Trouble*.

Inside, there were sticky traps around the California Pizza Kitchen logo. A single unicorn was stuck to one, struggling to pull its hooves free, but it only got more stuck.

Wolf unsheathed the spike of surgical steel at the end of his spear and punched it between the unicorn's shoulder blades. He lifted it up and pried the unicorn off the sticky trap before sliding it off the spear into his containment bag and zipping it closed.

"'Lonzo?" I didn't see him.

"Aqui," came from what used to be the kitchen.

Alonzo stood on the counter peering up into one of the vents with a flashlight. His containment bag was already half-full and wriggling.

"Kit is getting shrink-wrap," I said.

He grunted an affirmative and his arm darted into the shadowy darkness of the vent only to reappear with a winged unicorn pierced on the end of his knife.

"How many?" I asked as he slid the unicorn into his bag.

"Eight so far. There're at least a few more fliers buzzing around."

Wolf peered under some shelving, spear at the ready. Excited shouts outside caused him to bang his head on the bottom of the shelf. "Crap."

I pulled out the walkie-talkie, "Report."

"Chaser has been sighted, Captain."

Oh, just peachy.

Alonzo took the unicorn spear out of my hand and jerked his head toward the door. "Go. We got this."

I reluctantly left them to finish on their own. *Get a grip, Kara. The situation is in capable hands. You don't need to supervise everything yourself.*

I took a deep breath.

'Do what must be done and find others to do the rest.' I could almost hear Dad say the words. It didn't matter how many times I roll them over in my head, I still felt like I should be doing more.

Across the street, the spotter on Macy's rooftop pointed east, her posture excited even at this distance.

I walked east on Camino De Rio Norte, shadowed by the airy tangle of barbed wire around the main mall complex. My people followed behind me at a distance. At the intersection of Camino De Le Reina and Camino Del Este, I wait. Overhead, in the eucalyptus trees, feral koalas descended from loosed zoo specimens placidly munched. The burned-out shells of an In and Out and a Taco Bell stood kitty corner. I heard the Chaser long before her three-wheeled motorcycle came into view with trailer bumping along behind it.

My heart brightened when I saw it was really her. My sister had survived another year in the wastes. Even at seven years my junior, no one would call her young. One of these years she would not return.

The Chaser stopped across the street and killed the bike's electric engine. She stepped off the bike flashing long, lean legs I would have envied four pregnancies and twenty odd years ago. She pulled off her helmet, revealing a face tanned to worn leather.

She really should have worn more sunscreen.

"Permission to enter Mission Valley, Captain?" she called across the distance.

"State your purpose," I returned, following the script.

My sister grinned. "Heard you were having a party."

I tried not to roll my eyes. "State your name, rank, and station."

"Jacey P. Caine, Chaser," she said loud enough for everyone to hear. "No station."

A murmur rippled through the crowd. They know Jacey, but it's always strange to hear someone declare 'No station.'

"You from Pendleton?" I say, trying to look suspicious. "Don't look much like a jarhead."

Jacey was silent for a moment, probably biting her tongue to keep from laughing.

I scowled convincingly at her. "'ren't from OB..." I made my voice dark, "not one of them hippies?"

Jacey almost lost it. She wiped a hand over her face to get control then raised both palms. "I am a Chaser, Captain. I live alone."

"What is your purpose in seeking entry to Mission Valley?"

Jacey grinned and motioned at the trailer behind her bike. "Goods to attend the festival and my services for a year's hospitality."

"Is there an honored guest for our festival?"

Jacey pulled the tarp off the trailer and the largest unicorn I had ever seen.

The crowd gasped.

The original Tarlow unicorns were tiny—the size of toys. Subsequent mutations had varied greatly—but the size had remained roughly the same with one notable exception; meat-eating unicorns had been getting steadily bigger over the years. The unicorn on Jacey's trailer was bigger than a Shetland pony, but not quite horse-sized. Its pearlescent horn was as long as my arm.

The unicorn stuck its head between the bars and extended a pink proboscis.

"Dios mios," someone said.

I had to agree. That was a huge goddamn unicorn.

I remembered myself and motioned towards the mall. "We welcome you, Chaser Jacey P. Caine."

* * *

The unicorn pen was set up outside the food court. There wasn't any food stored or prepared there, but we still called it the food court. Outside, everything glittered with unicorn dust blown in off the river. We ran air filters in buildings where people live or work, but the glittery powder got tracked in no matter what we did. We tried to keep the station swept, but there'd been a Santa Ana wind the last few days, coating everything in dried unicorn excretions.

Jacey used a sheathed spear to prod the unicorn into the center of the pen. Some of my people pulled away the trailer and closed the pen behind her. Jacey gave the unicorn a sharp jab and walked backwards to the edge of the pen.

"If you ever call me a hippy again," she warned, jumping the fence.

"I know, I know," I laughed.

She hugged me, "It's good to see you, Kara."

"How are you?"

She shrugged. "Still able to stagger." Jacey waved her spear at one of the kids climbing on the fence. "Careful, he's cranky. Getting ready to molt."

The kids jumped down and watched the unicorn a few paces further back.

I noticed my youngest among them. "Phin, you're supposed to be grinding chitin."

"Mom," he whined, "No one else is working."

"No one?" I asked in a voice encouraging him to rethink his words.

Phin made a noise to indicate he thought I was being unreasonable and unfair.

Jacey patted him on the head. "Hey, Phin. You're getting tall."

Phin put fists on his hips as he stared up at Jacey. "You should teach me to be Chaser."

Jacey looked to me for help.

I shrugged. *Knock yourself out, sis.*

She sighed and tried to pat him on the head again.

Phin leaned out of reach and stamped his foot. "You're probably gonna die soon. Who will be Chaser then? You have to teach me."

My sister gave me a beseeching look. I smiled and shook my head.

"You wanna be Chaser?" she asked.

Phin's face was all seriousness as he nodded.

"Tell me what you know about unicorns." Jacey's posture straightened and her eyes took on a hardness reminiscent of our father.

"They're attracted to water," said Phin, moving to an at-ease position. "Probably because Tarlow engineered 'em from water-bears."

Jacey nodded.

"People think they don't like light, but it's dry they don't like." Phin's face scrunched up as he tried to think. "They're really hard to kill unless you break open their chitin and even then it takes 'em awhile to die unless you smash 'em."

"That's it?" asked Jacey. "Where do they sleep? Eat? When do they mate? How do you find them? How do they find food?"

Phin bit his lip and looked down.

"How many unicorns have you speared all by yourself?" asked Jacey.

"Fifty-eight," mumbled Phin.

"When you've killed fifty-eight thousand and know everything about them, come ask again."

Phin frowned. "You'll be dead."

"Better kill 'em them fast, then."

I pointed over his shoulder toward the processing building. "Go."

"But," protested Phin.

"Go!"

"Yes, Captain." Phin spun on his heel and stomped off.

"Charming age," said Jacey.

"Watch yourself, or I'll send him home with you."

"I haven't even been here an hour," said Jacey. "You can't possibly be mad at me yet."

"Oh," I said, "you'll be here a few days. Plenty of time to get in trouble."

Jacey laughed and shook her head. "I could set the place on fire and you still wouldn't trust me with one of your cubs."

No, I wouldn't. Grief stitched through my heart. *You will never take anything of mine again.*

"Please tell me this beast of a unicorn didn't stumble into your camp," I said, changing the subject.

She shook her head, glancing around at the crowd, and leaned closer. "Sycuan has a ranch. Agreed to save him for me as long as I took him off their hands before fall."

My eyes widened in surprise. "Are they all that big?"

"Matters what you feed 'em." She gestured at the unicorn. "Tossed him a lion carcass a few months back and he's been molting bigger ever since."

CJ and his group arrived twenty minutes after everyone else. He looked troubled and his group was two people short.

I caught his gaze for a split second before he looked away and refused to look back. *Come talk to me*, I thought fervently in his direction. *Let me fix this.*

Commanders from other Green Line stations started laying out festival gifts inside the food court, to be shared between the stations.

Jacey rummaged in her saddlebags as we headed inside, pulling out several plastic packages of her own. She raised one over her head, "For your generous hospitality, People of the Green Line."

One of my lieutenant commanders picked up Jacey's packages and went to secure them in cold storage. The last thing we needed was for someone to accidentally drop five liters of unicorn pheromones. Two grams were enough to attract every unicorn for 500 yards—further with a good wind. One package was enough to supply all of our perimeter traps for a year.

Alonzo slipped in and sat down next to me with a peck on the cheek. "I think we got them all."

"Good." I put my hand in his. "Will you talk to Phin?"

Alonzo ran a hand through dark hair sparkling with dust. "What's my son done this time?"

Jacey chuckled.

I straightened Alonzo's collar. "He's not taking his demotion well. Maybe suggest he can do trap duty if he gets through a week of grinding without demerits?"

Alonzo leaned over to kiss me. "You could be the good cop every once in awhile, y'know."

"Maybe when he's older."

My partner's face took on exaggerated seriousness. "I can be bad cop."

"For about five minutes." I patted his thigh. "Go."

Alonzo laughed and got to his feet. "Yes, Captain." I swatted at him, but his long legs danced out of reach.

Jacey grinned at me. "You've got your work cut out for you, keeping up with that young buck."

I tried to squash a wave of anger and irritation. She of all people had no right to make comments about my choice of partners.

Her hands came up in a placating motion as she realized she'd overstepped—again. "I didn't mean…"

I sucked in an angry breath and said nothing as I moved to stand.

"Why won't CJ look this way?" asked Jacey. "Is it me? Are you fighting?"

I motioned at Wolf and Kit to bring the door from CPK to the center of the room.

"He has brought this on himself," I muttered.

Conversation tapered off.

"Drop it," I said.

A metallic booming sound echoed as the door hit the floor. There was silence.

"Our hospitality," I said, pitching my voice to carry, "has been repaid with thievery."

I let my words sink in amid gasps and low murmurs.

Every Commander met my gaze with outrage and astonishment. Everyone except CJ. A flush across his cheeks and ears wasn't hidden by his lowered gaze.

"Not just theft," I continued, "but they also left the storehouse open behind them."

I wasn't the only one watching CJ now. His two junior lieutenants were conspicuously absent, their guilt all but assured. I had warned him not to take those two, that they'd never done more than the bare minimum of work.

A woman with long hair the color of chocolate put a hand on CJ's arm. His eyes darted across the room to where Jacey sat. Anger flared deep inside me as CJ rose slowly to his feet, looking for all the world like his father did the day he deserted us.

"I…" CJ's voice cracked, reminding me my son, and not his father, stood before me. "I take responsibility for my crew." His gaze finally rose to meet mine.

"Why aren't they here to take responsibility themselves."

"We—" CJ stopped and corrected himself. "I didn't realize they'd gone until after Chaser Jacey arrived." He shifted to attention and lowered his eyes.

"I take full responsibility and will abide by any punishment you deem fit, Captain," said CJ.

Eighteen years ago, his father stood before me like this. Two children, seven years, and he needed Her to be happy. I'd been too numb, and grief-stricken from losing our daughter Luna only months before to do anything but nod dumbly as my husband told me he was leaving.

I stared down at my son. There was only one punishment for such blatant disregard of community welfare: exile.

I could not watch CJ disappear to the east like his father, never to be seen again.

"Let the unicorn decide." Jacey called out.

I wheeled on her, wishing for a spear to put in her gut.

She stayed out of my lunge range as she spoke. "If he sacrifices the beast, he proves himself still worthy of the Green Line. If I am forced to step in to save him, he will be exiled to the wastes."

A rumble of what sounded like agreement from the crowd kept me from denouncing the idea like I wanted to. I could just disband Fashion Valley. Bust CJ down to pollywog with Phin and force him to earn his way back up the ranks to Commander.

"I accept," said CJ before I could voice the idea in my head.

"No!" The chocolate-haired woman rushed forward to clutch at CJ. "We need you."

"Will you take my crew with no retribution and no loss of rank if I fail?" asked CJ.

I was stuck. If I didn't answer him, I risked letting his crew believe we wouldn't welcome them back. If I answered, I sent my son to fight a unicorn.

I never wanted to be Captain. My predecessor warned me never to trust anyone who wanted command—especially if that person was myself.

I glared at my sister, angry tears wetting my lashes. How dare she put my son in danger. The words to revoke her hospitality burned in the back of my throat.

"Please," CJ whispered. His fingers tangled with those of the chocolate-haired woman.

His eyes were clear turquoise. There was finally understanding in their bright depths. He stood here not because he wanted to lead, but because he must.

"Your crew is always welcome at Mission Valley with no loss of rank from their departure." I said.

CJ nodded.

"Their service at Fashion would be considered for future promotions as well."

His eyes widened, but he said, "I accept on behalf of Fashion Valley Station and await my challenge."

"Dismissed." The syllables felt like a mass of blades shredding their way out of my throat.

* * *

I took refuge in my room and awakened in the evening to find Phin curled up on the edge of my mattress watching me with dark eyes. I opened my arms and he snuggled in against me.

"Is CJ really going to fight the unicorn?"

I squeezed Phin closer and kissed the top of his sweat-damp hair.

He wriggled free. "Is CJ going to live here again if he kills the unicorn?"

"I don't know." I felt the weight of every elapsed second of my life pressing against my existence.

Phin sat up and patted my shoulder with a grubby hand. "It's the festival, Momma. Nothing bad can happen."

He slipped off the bed and was out of the room before I could think of anything to say.

* * *

In the food court, the festivities were underway. Carefully covered food trays held seasonal delicacies. Some of our long-hoarded drink mix had been made up into a watery punch of mostly color with a hint of fruit.

CJ and Jacey sat outside by the unicorn pen. She gestured toward a part of the unicorn's anatomy then made a jabbing or slashing motion. CJ nodded grimly.

The chocolate-haired woman sat by the window staring at them with arms crossed across her stomach, sun-shirt rolled up to the elbows, revealing the stretchy gray nausea bands on her wrists.

Oh.

I sat next to her and offered one of the hard candies made for the festival. "Here. It will help your stomach."

She unwrapped and put the candy in her mouth.

What was her name? Daria? No. Dora.

"Idiots," I muttered looking out at the unicorn pen.

"Por qué?" Dora finally turned toward me.

I gestured to Jacey and CJ. "If they'd waited a few more minutes, I would have offered the same courtesy for his people in exchange for a demotion. If he'd accepted with humility and worked hard, he'd be back to rank by spring."

Dora sighed. "Wouldn't work. He's humbled, but humility is still beyond his reach."

It was my turn to sigh. She was right. Even if it worked temporarily, CJ and I would clash just as explosively in the future, and we'd be back where we started, sans unicorn.

"I don't want him to fight that." I flung a hand at the unicorn.

Wolf had brought it a bucket of tilapia. The unicorn pierced each fish with its proboscis and sucked them dry.

"He'll fight no matter what we say," said Dora. "Stubborn fool."

I nodded. "He gets it from his mother."

This coaxed a small smile, but it disappeared almost immediately as her eyes flicked back to the unicorn.

"Captain?" she asked after a moment.

I shook my head. "Not Captain, just Kara. Two women discussing our shared interests."

Dora smiled again. "Then let us discuss how we might yet turn unicorns into lemonade."

* * *

After midnight, I found Jacey on the roof of Macy's Home sitting in a lawn chair, staring up at the stars.

"If you're going to hit me, I won't stop you," she said without taking her eyes off the sky.

"I didn't hit you then. What makes you think I'd do it now?"

"Don't give me that, Momma Bear. I saw the look in your eyes. You'd have gutted me where I stood this afternoon. He might be a Commander, but he's still your cub as much as Phin."

"A fact you seem to have forgotten."

"No." Jacey's voice was quiet.

"Other people might use your title as a mark of honor," I said, "but I still remember why you have it. CJ's not Chase."

"He's Chase's son."

"He's my son!" My voice echoed and I lowered it before continuing. "I know Chase hurt when Luna died. We all hurt. But I had to stand in the wreckage of my life and watch the two of you disappear to the east, with no answers for the son who wanted to know why Daddy left him behind. CJ and I have that hurt too. I have long forgiven, but I still remember and sometimes it still hurts."

I stared into the glint of Jacey's eyes. "CJ is still an angry young man. Do you really think he'll thank you when you step in to save him? Eventually, he'll realize you never had any intention of letting him succeed or fail. You're just a lonely old woman who wants a familiar face and when you look at him you're not even seeing the man that's there—just echoes of the one we lost."

The lawn chair squeaked as Jacey began to sob.

I knelt beside her and let my baby sister cry against my shoulder. I held her tight against the weight of all our years.

"You're always welcome here," I said.

She choked through her sobs, trying to get control. "We'd kill each other."

I wiped away my own tears. "Maybe, but you could visit more than once a year."

"And tomorrow?"

I squeezed her hand. "Tomorrow you will do nothing."

* * *

The first full day of Fiesta de Unicornios felt warm even before the sun reached the horizon. The unicorn looked dull and sluggish as Jacey prodded it into the trailer for its final trip. At 0700 we rang the alarm, and at 0730 the People of the Green Line—from skirt-clinging barnacles and wee pollywogs all the way to Commanders and Captain—walked. Every able-bodied crewmember carried a spear and at least one containment bag. Teenage cadets walked the trolley tracks to estimate numbers while the rest of us headed down Camino Del Rio Norte to the stadium.

It wasn't a great distance, less than three miles, but with little legs among the group it took nearly two hours. The cadets beat us handily and waited beside the fallen scoreboard.

Jacey's bike led the procession onto the field. Tattered and faded signs for the Aztecs and their sponsors still adorned the stands. Dry mudcracks crunched underfoot as we moved across the empty field.

My sister parked the trailer opening facing what used to be the visitor's bench and unhooked it from the bike.

The elder officers formed a human chain to prevent the unicorn from escaping through the scoreboard hole while everyone else moved to the relative safety of the fifty-yard line seating.

Jacey pulled the tarp off to groans and curses. The unicorn had molted during the journey. It seemed a little bigger, its chitin shell glimmering and sparkling white, and its horn a delicate pink that matched the probing proboscis and eyes.

Jacey attached a long rope to the quick release on the back of the trailer.

I took the rope out of her hands. "You're going to sit in the stands."

"Don't be stupid," Jacey hissed. "You need me down here in case something goes wrong."

"Trust me." I grabbed her arm. "Whatever happens, I need you to keep Phin in the stands."

She stared at me before climbing up next to Wolf and Phin. "Don't make me regret this."

CJ and I stood alone on the field. He adjusted the large knife sheathed on his thigh and wiped his hands on his pants before accepting the spear from me.

I gave his arm a little squeeze and turned to the crowd. "People of the Green Line, this man failed to prevent theft and wanton endangerment perpetrated by members of his crew. If the unicorn fails to die by his hand, he shall be stripped of all rank and banished to wastes." I turned to CJ. "Commander Chase Packard Junior, do you accept these terms?"

"Wait!" Dora and the Fashion Valley crew surged forward onto the field. "If he must pay for crimes of his crew, as his crew must be allowed to share in his trial."

Wolf and Kit jumped down to Dora's side, followed by Alonzo, several of my Jr. Lieutenants, and a handful of cadets.

"He is a Commander of the Green Line," said Wolf unsheathing his spear, "and my brother."

Alonzo shrugged sheepishly, fooling no one. "We support him." It wasn't what we'd agreed he would say, but it worked.

"Do you all accept the terms of the trial?"

A chorus of voices yelled, "Aye."

Kit grinned at CJ. "What are your orders, Commander?"

That shook CJ out of his daze, and he arranged half his troops in a staggered corridor with himself at the end. The unicorn sensed something had changed and began to kick at the trailer gate. CJ moved the rest of us in front of the stands, ready to lend aid.

"Hurry up," urged Jacey. She restrained Phin from jumping on the field by his hair.

"Ready!" yelled CJ. "Release!"

The door swung open and the unicorn charged into a forest of spears. Within seconds, it was skewered in place from both sides.

"Hold your position." CJ stepped forward, caught the unicorn's horn in one hand, pushed it up and back as he sank the knife to the handle in the beast's neck. He strained to wiggle the blade back and forth and finally wrenched it outward through the unicorn's neck with a sound like splitting a melon. Pink pearlescent liquid gushed from the wound and a sweet, almost cotton candy smell filled the air.

"Clear!" yelled CJ.

Everyone with a spear in the beast let go and fell back to in front of the stands.

It staggered five or six steps in the opposite direction and collapsed to the dirt.

"Clear the way!" I yelled. "Douse Commander Packard in vinegar."

My officers scrambled into the bleachers and circle around the stadium towards us, warily watching the gap. Dora and Kit poured gallons of vinegar over CJ and anyone else speckled with droplets of pink liquid.

"They're coming!" called the spotters on the upper ring of the stadium.

Soon a moving carpet of tiny unicorns rippled into view in the parking lot beyond.

The original Tarlow unicorns reproduced with parthenogenesis—all female and their offspring basically clones. Given a plentiful food supply, they still reproduced that way. After the great die-off, when most of the plants were gone, they started producing the occasional pink-horned male. In late fall, males ceased to eat, drink or sleep and started releasing pheromones from a pouch in their necks. They mated until they died of exhaustion or starvation.

Sounded like a good way to go, until you saw it—unicorns barely able to stand, eyes dull and lifeless, nothing there but instinct. I saw a male with half its side gone from a turtle bite, but still going as life oozed out over its pearly flank.

Every year, we sacrificed a male unicorn to ensure our main unicorn harvest. A pheromone pouch on a unicorn this big? We'd run out of containment sacks long before we ran out of unicorns. Back at the station, the unicorns will be shelled and their meat processed. Phin would have his work cut out running the grinder to process the leftover shells into hydroponic medium.

I hugged CJ. "Congratulations, Commander."

"CJ did land the killing blow," Dora said conversationally. "Does that mean he can claim a hospitality boon like the Chaser?"

Oh, you clever little minx. I liked this girl.

"Seems fair to me," contributed Jacey, climbing down to the field.

"What do you have in mind?" I asked Dora.

"The right to overwinter at Mission Valley for the flood months, at our Fashion ranks," Dora stated without hesitation. "In the spring we'll return to our own station."

"Granted," I said, shaking Dora's hand.

Phin jumped in front of us to spear one of the unicorns racing ahead of the pack. "Fifty-nine!" He slid it off the spike into his bag with a smug nod and promptly stabbed another. "Sixty!"

* * *

Captain's Log 8-28-57 0030
Thanks to Chaser Jacey's unicorn and Lt. Commander Dora, we had our most successful harvest in history. Things may have gone a little pear-shaped for humanity after unicorns destroyed the world, but we're still here. It's going to take more than a bunch of little pon—

Alonzo turned off the light.
"Hey, I'm—"
He silenced my complaints with a kiss. "Hmm?"
I gave in. "—never going to finish an entry."

Minerva Zimmerman lived in San Diego for five years. She misses California Burritos and crispy chile rellenos most of all. Now she lives in rainy rural Oregon, spending her days amid remnants of our past civilizations and their current dangers. Her property could become self-sufficient in the event of an apocalypse, but is currently performing below potential.

Trading with the Ruks

By
Nathan Shumate

    Malachi and his partners met the Ruk caravan at the trading hill outside the village. A single sweaty, nervous Ruk herald had come into the village square to announce the wagon train's approach, and then he had scrabbled away as fast as his bandy legs could carry him. The hill was far enough away from the settlement to be hidden by the rolling land, though the village was no secret; one only had to follow the wagon ruts back from the trading hill, as the lone herald Ruk had done. But mutant tribes were never invited into a village of the Pure, not with the rumors and reports of maidens spirited away by various mutant caravans to help keep their deformed races alive.

    Then there was the fact that Ruks stank. Malachi steeled himself and kept from flinching as a Ruk from the caravan, evidently its trade captain, climbed to the crest of the trading hill and bowed. He was dressed, like all those in the caravan, in a plain tunic of scavenged fabric that reached to his knobby knees. As the wind changed, the smell of him caught Malachi like a fist to the side of the head: sour and dank, like wine that had turned to vinegar, mixed with mushrooms. Malachi's polite smile never faltered, even as he heard his partners behind him shift and cough.

"Welcome to trade, caravaneer," Malachi said formally. "I am Malachi, Asael's son."

"Many thanks for your welcome," the Ruk said. "I am Skuchi Var-Bel Frashaa."

Malachi wondered idly if he had met this particular Ruk at a previous year's trade. He never remembered their names, given only as a formality, and they all looked the same to him: short like a child, with a bald and square head squatting neckless on lumpy shoulders, a potbelly pushing the tunic forward, and spindly arms poking out of the armholes to end in spadelike fingers that hung fully to the knees. This one, this Skuchi, had a necklace of horses' teeth and twisted bits of metal, probably to show his status as chief trader for the caravan.

Two lieutenants lingered on the slope of the hill; the rest of the Ruks hung back at the bottom with their wagons, their various beasts of burden stomping and whinnying. Skuchi folded himself to the ground and motioned to his lieutenants, who hurried forward, spread a blanket before him, and dropped several wrapped bundles before retreating. Malachi's men did the same, setting covered baskets before him on the blanket they unrolled.

Sitting, Malachi didn't have nearly the advantage of height over the Ruk, and they saw almost eye to eye. Skuchi smiled, showing the gapped, rounded teeth common to all Ruks, and Malachi had a sudden vision of this Ruk or one like it slavering over a winsome maid. He pushed this afterimage of old wives' tales out of his mind.

"Let us trade," Malachi said.

* * *

The trade items were as expected. The Pure had grain and dried beans, cheese, and a few homespun blankets and bolts of cloth. This village was also renowned for a master flute-maker and his apprentices, but Malachi knew not to bother bringing those wares up to the trading hill. Of the mutant peoples, only the Glossae had any sense or appreciation of music. Even then their tastes were so alien that only instruments made specifically for Glossae use interested them, and the village flute-maker refused to profane his craft to that end.

The Ruks had implements and materials scavenged from the dead zones, areas the Pure wouldn't enter for fear of infertility or mutation. They offered metal cooking pots and glass bowls, intact or mostly so, cables of copper and other materials with which the villagers could swap out perishable twine or leather for lashings, and some few garments and footwear, though usable examples of each were getting rarer. Some ornaments and oddities caught his eye, but in his early years Malachi had learned through hard experience never to barter for something whose utility wasn't obvious, no matter what the Ruks promised.

They shared fresh beer from the village as they traded and by midday had cleared their wares. Malachi's men loaded the Ruks' new foodstuffs onto their caravan, and the Ruks filled the villagers' empty wagons, though not wholly.

At last, Malachi got stiffly to his feet as his men cleaned up his blanket. His lower back ached, and his head thumped with the heat of the sunlight and the beer. Skuchi hopped up like a frog.

"It is always a pleasure, Malachi," the Ruk said. "These many years, you have been a fair and friendly partner in trade."

At least the Ruks can tell *us* apart, Malachi thought. "I am honored," Malachi replied. "And I always look forward to your appearance in trading season." The heat of the sun had not improved the Ruk's stench, and Malachi wished that the wind would change.

Skuchi glanced behind Malachi to where his men were securing their purchases. "I have something for you, as one of our favorite traders," he said in a lower voice. "I did not bring it out earlier because I didn't want it to become an item of trade. It is a gift."

"Really?" Malachi was too late in hiding his surprise. Ruks were known for being forthright traders, not for their generosity. The last of the beer had been drunk an hour before, and Malachi's mouth was coated with dry stickiness.

"Please, keep this to yourself," Skuchi said, holding up a broad-fingered hand. "We Ruks have a reputation to uphold. Is there any way you can dismiss your men without arousing suspicion?"

Malachi's chest puffed up. He had already been steeling himself for a week of muttered complaints from those who thought that he hadn't gained as much advantage in the trade as they thought reasonable. Not that any of *them* volunteered for the duty. No, they just assumed from their comfortable homes that they would trade more keenly with the stinking Ruks. Well, at least someone appreciated his efforts at barter, and if it wasn't one of the Pure, well, a gift was a gift.

Malachi descended the hill halfway and called to his men, "Ho! The Ruks want me to help them with their maps! Go on without me!"

The men signaled assent, and Malachi returned to where Skuchi was waiting. "Come," Skuchi said, "we have kept it at the caravan."

Malachi followed the trollish mutant down the side of the hill, realizing with a start that he was going to be closer to the Ruk caravan than he had ever been. He had never been so close to so many Ruks, either. The various wagons were moving into single file for traveling, their beasts of burdens as varied as the vehicles they pulled: open wagons, two-wheeled carts, wagons with fabric tents suspended above, and some which were like boxes on wheels, constructed of scavenged wood. The air got thick with Ruk-stench as they wound among the wagons, and Malachi found that even breathing through his mouth didn't help overmuch; instead, he fancied he could taste the stink.

Following Skuchi, he rounded a wagon that was wholly enclosed, with window spaces and a low doorway covered with shutters that barred from the outside. He half-wondered if locked wagons like this contributed to the tales of Ruk-abducted maidens. Then he saw something out of the corner of his eye, something aimed toward his head.

It struck before he could defend himself, and the world whirled into haze and blackness.

* * *

Malachi only realized that he was approaching consciousness again because of the smell. He had thought he knew how bad Ruk-smell could be, but wherever he was now, the stink in his nostrils was so thick it almost choked the air from his lungs. He was afraid to open his eyes because the stench might actually be thick enough to see.

He shifted his arms, intending to cradle his aching head, but his arms wouldn't move; they were held out away from his body by something tied around his wrists. His ankles, too, were held immobile, away from his body. His eyes opened, despite the promised pain, and he found himself in a small boxlike space, unlit except by dim light creeping between ill-fitting boards. The floor of the box was covered with filthy straw. His arms and legs were gripped by manacles of materials from the Long Ago, metal and wire cobbled together with less identifiable substances.

As his vision cleared gradually, he looked again at the space that held him, at the shuttered windows and low door, and realized that he was inside the wagon he had noticed right before—before what? Before he was attacked, obviously. But why?

The door at the far end opened. Beyond, it was night, with the glare of an unseen fire reflecting inside; he had obviously been unconscious for hours, long enough for the caravan to have moved far from the village. How long before anyone in the village would become suspicious?

The doorway was filled with the silhouette of a Ruk clambering inside. The door was closed from the outside, and Malachi could hear the bar dropping. Then the Ruk uncovered a lantern, and the yellow light fell upon a necklace of horses' teeth and metal around the Ruk's neck.

"I'm glad to see you awake," Skuchi said. "I had half-feared that I had struck you too hard."

"S…Skuchi?" Malachi mumbled, finding that his mouth was still sluggish.

"At last, you remember me!" Skuchi said, mouth distended in a wide, grotesque smile. "Every year, I can tell that I am new to you. Perhaps all Ruks look alike to you, heh?"

In his other hand, Skuchi held a small box made from more materials from Long Ago. He extended it with his long spidery arm and flipped it open with a blunt thumb. Malachi couldn't see what was inside it, but vapors fairly leapt out, a different smell. It was piercing instead of cloying, sharp instead of bludgeoning. Malachi felt a wave of dizziness and heard his blood pounding in his temples, his neck, his whole body. Skuchi flipped the box closed, and Malachi lay there with his breath coming in gasps, his heart thumping, sweat starting out all over his body.

Skuchi set the box and the lantern down in the far corner of the wagon. "You are one of our favorite traders," he crooned, "certainly *my* favorite trader. And this is how we show our favor."

With both hands he lifted the lower edge of his tunic. Unable to look away, Malachi saw the protruding belly exposed, and beneath it, where he had assumed to see a mutated version of his own manhood…he saw nothing.

And against his will he understood.

Skuchi held the tunic up beneath his—beneath *her* arms. "You have much we will take in trade, my sisters and I," she chuckled.

Malachi was gasping too convulsively even to scream.

Nathan Shumate has wasted over a decade of his life as a media critic, chiefly reviewing genre and B-movies at the website coldfusionvideo.com. He is also the editor of the magazine/anthology *Arcane* at arcanemagazine.com, and has written screenplays, comic book scripts, and novels, some of which he's even gotten paid for. He blogs and putters at nathanshumate.com.

Midwife

by
Jon-Michael Emory

Princeton and Penelope swam concertedly in tight circles, conversing spiritedly in anticipation, a volley of clicks and high-pitched barks echoing through the clear, cerulean water. Their permanently-affixed smiles appeared even wider this morning, and it was no wonder. Something whispered in them, an inkling in their warm blood that today was *The Day*.

* * *

Amanda pattered along the beach, the white granular sand wet and warm beneath her bare feet. She lifted the hem of her scarlet cotton pinafore from the waves as she went, curtsying to the crystalline tide.

A feeling of great expectation nursed her stride; a maternal goading that was stronger than anything she had ever felt before. She glanced back at the house, hoping that Matthew would be there, running from the porch, racing like hell to catch up with her. But she knew he was gone, and not due back until later that morning.

Still, she hoped… A father should not miss the birth of his first child.

Finding Home

    The cove where Princeton and Penelope waited was rimmed with jagged, centuries-worn rock; a colonnade of black volcanic dregs that contrasted sharply, aesthetically, against the white sands and turquoise waters of the island. Nine hundred-foot Fertility Poles rose from the stones, flying either a blue or pink pennant to represent each child born in the sacred inlet. Amanda had been born there twenty-nine years before, as had her mother before her. And she was grateful to Matthew for having purchased the island, and for ultimately conceding to her wishes to live there.

    The ninth pennant, last in the procession and pink in color, flew at half-mast.

    She was almost there.

    Two gulls cawed and careened above her, imploring her to move faster. *Faster.*

* * *

    Princeton nudged Penelope gently with his rostrum, prodding her toward shallower water. Air bubbles, like a string of crystal beads, arose from her blowhole as she clicked and whistled in obedience. She propelled herself forward with a quick thrust of her tail.

    Princeton did not accompany her, but instead remained at the mouth of the cove. Like the rest of the pod farther out, he would now stand guard, and wait.

* * *

    Amanda stopped, inhaled deeply, and then rapidly articulated a series of clicks and squeaks. Penelope answered immediately from the cove.

    Amanda smiled and continued on.

    Her thoughts veered back to Matthew. Her husband had not been born like her. His had been a rare birth, the kind that separated him from the majority and placed him, and those few like him, into the extreme upper echelons of ruling mankind. He did not have a title, such as President or King, like the world leaders had hundreds of years before him, but was simply referred to by the people as 'Matthew.'

He had been *Borne of Woman.*

And Amanda knew that had her husband been born as she, he would never have left this morning, but would have been constrained by the same innate forces that now drove her unyieldingly across the white, gleaming shore.

She reached reassuringly into the pocket of her gown. The conch handles of the scissors were so smooth and silky that they felt wet to the touch. She quickened her pace.

* * *

The tip of Penelope's dorsal fin sliced the water. A shimmering latticework of morning sunshine rollicked on her back as she glided gracefully inward, just below the surface. Something as powerful as instinct compelled her; a cognitive alliance with the Midwife, a kind of telepathic tethering that had evolved in both of their kind through centuries of subrogation. Only those humans *Borne of Woman* lacked the connection.

Throughout her pregnancy, Penelope had considered with much sorrow that human condition that prevented nearly every adult female the ability to carry a fetus to term, and that the human race might have long ago vanished had it not been for her species' willingness to continue its propagation.

It was an honor among her kind to be chosen a Surrogate Mother, and she was feeling especially proud today. Being only two years old, this would be her first child. The gestation cycle was very near its end.

And she was excited.

She was also very afraid—not of failing maternally, but of having to surrender the baby. This eventuality had concerned her greatly for the past ten months; from the moment the embryo was implanted in her womb.

She rose, filling her lungs with air.

* * *

Finding Home

As she neared the craggy periphery, Amanda was suddenly overcome with profound gratitude and admiration. It wasn't until that very moment when she realized just how deep and far-reaching her feelings were for Penelope. Their many months of preparation before and after the embryo's implantation had been spent bonding, getting to know one another, developing a relationship that would ultimately ensure mutual respect and support. They had built a solid friendship, one founded upon faith and trust and hope, and one that would live in their hearts for the rest of their lives.

Amanda winced as she imagined what it must have been like five hundred years ago, before The Dawn of Sentience. Some surrogate dolphins had to be destroyed immediately following delivery because their fierce maternal instincts would not allow them to peacefully surrender the newborn. And the ones that weren't killed were often later found dead upon the shore, having beached themselves over the agonizing loss of the child. Amanda sighed, thankful that she and Penelope were of a wiser and more appreciative chapter in history, and not prone to such destructive ways.

She walked between two boulders, stepped into the warm shallows and, with a hand shielding her brow, perused the immediate waters.

* * *

Penelope slipped furtively through the cove, dodging, eluding, hesitating. The moment she had for so long anticipated was at hand, and the one fear that had loitered in the periphery of her happiness for the past ten months was now emerging as a much more powerful and seductive force than she had ever imagined, eclipsing all other emotions with its black, envious shadow.

She cried out to Princeton, craving his closeness, desperately needing his strong, soothing body next to hers, demanding his *understanding*. She was scared and sad and suddenly feeling very alone.

Princeton and the rest of the pod replied with cajoling song.

Penelope swam closer to shore, then retreated. She was flustered, confused... The human to whom she had grown so close—who waited devotedly in the shallows—was now a threat.

* * *

Sensing Penelope's newfound reluctance, Amanda began uttering consoling clicks from deep within her throat, while slapping the water with both hands; signals she'd often used in the past to summon her friend. She was not overly concerned. It was common for a Surrogate Mother to display some apprehension in those last minutes, just before delivery; it was expected, in fact.

Amanda, slightly nauseous over the fluttering of her own butterflies, sympathized. She had never before been a Midwife; had never even been a bystander to such a hallowed event.

She continued to beat the water, reassuring herself that things would be just fine.

Just fine.

* * *

The hot, sharp pangs of labor steadily grew until she could no longer tarry in her indecision. And as she pushed herself away from the deeper waters of the cove, the reality of her burden—the true reason why she'd accepted the responsibility initially—returned to her heart in its old guise of selfless acquiescence. She suddenly remembered that the baby she was carrying was not hers, but belonged to a dear and wonderful friend; a female who, unlike herself, could not sustain life within her own womb.

With restored commitment Penelope continued toward the shallows, steering gracefully now; purposefully.

She broke the surface and warbled a song that sounded both happy and sad.

* * *

    Amanda excitedly removed the scissors from her pocket, then pulled the gown over her head, tossing it to shore. Naked, she waded up to her hips, reached out, and then dove. The warmth of the water soothed her soul as well as her skin, inducing tranquility like a warm blanket induces sleep. She found herself coveting the water again, wishing the milieu of weightless air to which she was prisoner was as buoyant and embracing. She often pined for the water; although always nearby in excess, she could only regress to it briefly, indulge in its sweet, peaceful medium for only moments at a time. It was her second home, stolen from her at birth by awkward, landlocked limbs.
    She rose, filling her lungs with air.

* * *

    His query went unanswered. Concerned, Matthew walked from the kitchen into the living room and again called out her name. Amanda was gone, but something lingered in her vacancy, wafting through the house, rousing his senses like a piquant fragrance of feminine extract. It *tingled*. He called out again, and was suddenly alerted to his own excitement, hearing it in his own voice as it echoed through the empty chambers of the house.
    He smiled, shouted victoriously, then ran for the door.

* * *

    Something like an ethereal strand of rope had lassoed Princeton, and growing more taut with each passing minute, tugging at him with emotional ferocity. He wanted to be with Penelope, could feel her need for him, and it was all he could do to remain with the pod, and wait.
    Then something resonated across his highly-sensitive skin; vibrations originating from farther out at sea. The others had felt them, too, and were already scattering to form a protective net. Princeton and three other males immediately

assembled, then dashed defensively toward the source of the sounds.

* * *

Amanda frantically waved to Matthew, who was still a ways down the beach but running with everything he had.
She could see the smile on his face; as bright as the sun.
She began slapping the water again, more forcefully this time; a cadence that resounded with anticipation.

* * *

It was a black, formidable shape, one of which Princeton was very familiar. And it cruised swiftly toward the shallower waters of the cove, lured by the cudgeling sounds coming from there; sounds that it no doubt mistook for an animal in distress. Princeton knew that it would very soon smell the blood of birth, and once it did it would be almost impossible to stop.
Delirious with fear, he swam faster, moving ahead of the other males.
It had to be killed.

* * *

Penelope swam close, then circled, wanting—needing—Amanda to stroke her skin, to soothe her with soft, comforting words, to ease her fiery pain.
She sensed that something was wrong farther out; an approaching threat. Then she heard the anxious cries from her kind, felt their nervous resonations in the water.
But her situation forced her to remain.
She slowed, then listed slightly, as if the bulge in her belly was more ballast than she could handle. She looked up at her friend with grateful eyes, then cooed like a baby.

* * *

At the Fertility Pole, Matthew breathlessly awaited the signal that would allow him to send the pink pennant to the top.

* * *

It was time.

With two quick thrusts of her tail, she darted out a ways, then turned and started slowly back. It was important to deliver the baby as close to the Midwife as possible, so bonding could begin instantaneously.

But this was her baby!

No, no, it wasn't.

But…

She began to push.

* * *

Moving at tremendous speed, Princeton struck the shark just below its left eye, his rostrum sending the animal off-course, but only slightly.

Quickly, and in synchronized succession, the other three males struck at the creature, at or near the same sensitive area, managing to stun it. Momentarily paralyzed, the shark slowly descended into the blue-blackness, then suddenly twitched back to life, resuming its earlier course without delay.

* * *

The baby arrived in a cumulus of blood.

Amanda caught her daughter, and with her free hand quickly began stroking Penelope's belly to hasten placental delivery, a formality, she felt, that was probably more ritualistic than it was necessary. But, surprisingly, it appeared to work, as the placenta soon emerged, followed by another red-grey cloud.

With the scissors, Amanda severed the cord two inches from the newborn's belly, and then gently guided her submerged daughter through the water, freeing her skin of the blood and mucosal tissue.

She thought she'd never in her life felt anything as smooth and wonderful as her baby's skin; even silkier than Penelope's.

"She's beautiful!" she shouted to Matthew, then began to cry.

* * *

Hands fast upon the halyard, Matthew hoisted the pennant to the gold finial, its final and most coveted destination.

His own eyes began to tear. He was now a father.

* * *

The birth complete, Penelope swam out a few yards, where she lingered with her thoughts, already heartsick over having surrendered her baby so easily. Yes, *her* baby! It was hers, by all rights! How could she have relinquished her child so effortlessly? Without so much as a voiced objection?

The newborn needed her desperately, didn't it? Didn't it?

Yes, she could feel its need. But her rational side told her that the baby could not survive in her world. It was not meant to. And this only intensified her despair.

She now loathed the woman whom she once called friend. A woman she would now and forever call thief!

These leaden emotions deepened her exhaustion; slowed her progress through the water to nearly a crawl. The drawing threat farther out—the safety of her school, of Princeton—did not concern her now. All she wanted to do was float. Drift.

Die.

She lifted her head from the water and made faint, lamenting sounds; weak, imploring cries that fell upon no one. No one at all.

Her ceaseless smile dichotomously remained.

Finding Home

* * *

Finally defeated, the shark fell slowly, quivering with spasms, as its brain sent frantic, jerky orders to its muscles.

Another shape descended alongside it; dead. Blood rose from Princeton's gaping wounds like smoke, drifting in a sky of water.

Tired and wounded, sick with grief, the three remaining males started back toward their pod, their mates.

They had lost a dear friend.

* * *

Amanda cradled the baby in her arms as she stepped from the waves. Matthew soon joined her, joy and astonishment seizing his face as he gazed down upon his beautiful daughter.

Amanda smiled. She had performed well as a Midwife, and felt that Penelope had demonstrated equal courage. She paused and turned to the water, making appreciative clicking noises within her throat. But Penelope did not answer; was nowhere to be seen.

Concern for her friend momentarily captured her, but was quickly reduced to an evanescent troubling that finally conceded to the sounds and needs of her baby.

A smile returned once more, then Penelope and Matthew gathered up her pinafore. They grew smaller down the shore, finally disappearing from view like hope sometimes does.

* * *

Penelope longed to swim in the sea of stars above her; to glide gracefully in that black medium where Princeton now swam.

On her side, moonlight setting her skin aglow, she softly cried to the night.

Waves nipped at her tail, the sand of the beach like so many tiny teeth against her sensitive skin.

Then the blackness that suspended those stars suddenly descended like a shaft of ebony light, and engulfed her. And she was there.

"Midwife" was first published in *Year 1: A Time of Change* (September, 1996), by Pirate Writings Publishing. Tom Piccirilli & Edward J. McFadden, Editors.

Jon-Michael Emory began his writing career twenty years ago as a lyricist for a small music company, DSM Producers, in New York City. On a whim, his producer called him one day and asked if he wrote anything "literary," that since she was on Publisher's Row, she could shop a sample around. He told her that he did, in fact, just recently finish a short story, and he sent it along. That story eventually won him "Featured Author" in a small magazine called *Heart Attack*, and he's been writing ever since. His fiction has appeared in magazines and anthologies such as *Next Phase*, *Night Terrors*, *Best of Millennium Sci Fi and Fantasy*, *New Genre II*, *Wired Hard III*, and the upcoming anthologies *Tales of Salt and Sorrow* and *Alternate Dimensions* from Static Movement Press.

Girl with Sunrise in Her Hair

By
Val Muller

From *Prophecies of The Great Wu-Shen Kulkulcan*:
Your lives are small, your numbers few. Together is our strength. Your life belongs to each of us, and to me. You who would deprive us of it by suicide, abandonment, or disobedience are but dishonorable thieves. In the time Before, you thought you were gods. Your materialism was sin: the flood was your punishment. You survived because you can obey—and, through service, redeem yourselves in the old ways. Those who think to leave my protection deserve the flooded world that awaits.

Sonja
30 June 2020
To My Son—

    I am running away from the Dome, but I am not a thief, despite what the Emperor may tell you. I want this journal to prove that, to show you my past and my hope for your future. Most Citizens treat the Emperor like a god. But not me. I can't forget what used to be. I can't accept the Emperor.

    Son, the first ten years of my life I spent in another age, a paradise and a burden you will never know. The Emperor does not allow us to speak of it. We made light by touching the wall.

We made water by turning a lever. These things made us gods, but they also distracted us from what was important. I know that now.

    The Great Wu-Shen Kulkulcan blames us. If we long for what we lost, he says, we will only lose ourselves once again. Maybe that's why I'm running away. Not a day goes by I don't think of the old world.

    Maybe I am lost.

* * *

From *Prophecies of The Great Wu-Shen Kulkulcan*:
Each of you was saved by divine hand for divine purpose. Mine is the voice of the divine. I am the all-seeing eye, the eternal serpent's cunning, the flying bird's perspective. Sacred knowledge flows through my veins. Heed me and prosper.

Prosper together.

Sonja
8 July 2020
My Dear Son—

    As I feel you growing inside me, I must tell you of my childhood. I write in secret and pray these charcoal scratches will last until you can read them—and that no Preceptor will confiscate the journal.

    I was born in a place you'll never find: the world has shifted since. I lived with my parents and little brother Peter. We lived near a lake with a dog called Igloo, who we rescued from a snow bank. Snow: something you may never know. When the land shifted, my cold home became the warm equator.

    In the old world, I would not have been bound by the hardships of a Citizen within the Dome. But in this stronghold against untamed nature, we must obey Wu-Shen Kulkulcan.

How can I make you see that it was not always so? That it doesn't have to be this way? How can I teach you to be the leader I know you can be?

I feel so alone—

But now, footsteps in the hall—

Ye
4 Cib 19 Tzec

During these lonely nightly rounds, I have only myself to talk to. And I usually talk about Sonja.

My feelings for her go against Wu-Shen's teachings. She is a lowly Citizen; I'm a Preceptor. Still, I'm drawn to her. We are among the youngest of the survivors, she and I—each saved as just children.

I noticed Sonja the first day they brought her here: the girl with sunrise in her hair, the girl from the red tunnel. Wu-Shen tried to give her a new name, but she wouldn't have it. All the others, so grateful to be saved, gladly accepted his name and pledged him their lives. They wore his clothing and cut their hair. They learned to count the days as Kulkulcan did. But little Sonja would do none of those things.

She had long hair, bright as the sunrise that used to drench the world in orange warmth. As a boy, I watched the sun rise every morning from my window high up in the apartment in a city whose name I no longer remember. But I must not speak of Before. Wu-Shen helped me to forget. By the time Sonja arrived, we hadn't seen the sun for months. Her hair reminded me of it.

But the shaman-emperor forbids long hair. They cut three small locks before Sonja kicked her way free and escaped to the edge of the Dome. I found her hunched between two fallen trees. She was crying, the tears shining red on her face in Dome light. She trembled when I touched her arm. We were still learning each other's languages, but I made her understand: she had to cut her hair or Wu-Shen would not let her stay. We could see through the Dome's red barrier. Where the floodwaters receded, the ground was smoldering and ashen. In other places, the floodwaters still washed against the Dome's translucent wall. Leaving the Dome meant death.

Sonja sat on the fallen log and stared straight into my eyes. She let me cut off her locks of hair…the whole time, she never took her eyes off me. Her hair fell around her feet in patterns, the way rays of sunshine used to fall on the floor of a leafy forest…

Now, I make my rounds, checking on the sleeping Citizens. Bodies sprawled on floor mats, exhausted from the day's labors. In the women's room, one figure stirs. One figure who always sleeps in the light spilling in from the hallway. Sonja. Restlessness haunts her. She tucks something under her pillow as she sees me. I nod.

She'll creep into the hallway. Follow me to the Preceptors' room. In the darkness, then, I will take Sonja, secretly and serenely.

* * *

From *Prophecies of The Great Wu-Shen Kulkulcan*:
The divine will not allow fertility in those not pure of heart. All of you, childless as stone, look deep within yourselves for the cause. This barren plague can only be cured by the Divine. Accept me as the voice of divinity, accept me completely to banish your flaws. Any who bears a child shall live in privilege in my palace under the protection of my Preceptors and myself.

Sonja
10 July 2020

Son, your father is a good man, but his loyalties are split. His heart belongs to me, but the shaman-emperor has captured his mind. I am afraid to tell him about you…but I will do so tonight. Will this be the last thing I write? I don't know how Ye will react, neither to you nor to my plan to leave the Dome.

I had a friend once, Hsing Wen Hsu. We did everything together. But a few years ago, she tried to run away. The Dome was still open back then, and she planned to find her way back home. I told her it was foolish. Even if she made the difficult journey, there would be nothing left of her home. She didn't listen.

Hsing Wen was gone a full two days before they counted her missing. They spent the third day searching the entire Dome. Two days after that, they found her in the jungle. Afterwards, we saw her only once. She was tightly bound and being dragged back into the Dome and into Wu-Shen's pyramid. A sliding panel opened at the lower level. The stone slabs echoed low and deep like a demon as they consumed Hsing Wen.

We never see anyone after they enter the pyramid. Will they take me there when they learn of you, Son? I can't keep you a secret, Son. Signs of you will soon be visible. Weight gain has caused others to be taken into the pyramid. But I would rather die than live under Wu-Shen's constant gaze. Of all the citizens to be blessed with a child, why me? The one who hates the Emperor! The one who looks so different, with red hair and large green eyes!

Hopefully, you will never experience life in the Dome...not as I have. Not if my plan works. But I fear they will take you before the end. You must understand that Wu-Shen Kulkulcan expects our gratitude; if you ever see him, you must obey his every demand—or at least seem to.

Seem to. That is the key.

Though I hate to admit it, there is some truth to his madness: he did actually save us. For me, it was a cold winter evening. Igloo and I walked out to the frozen lake. I was bundled up in the lonely cold, even though my parents didn't want me out in such bitterness. All I had was this little pink flashlight and a tin of gingerbread cookies (a type of food, sweeter than anything in the Dome). The cookies were shaped like people, and I ate one, starting at the feet. When nothing but the head remained, I kept looking at its candy eyes. This must seem silly to you. It was just a cookie, after all. Still, I imagined that it felt sad. I couldn't bring myself to eat its eyes: they were all it had left. Suddenly I felt sad about being away. I wanted to go home where it was warm, to be with my family.

I called for Igloo, but the ground around me shook. A tunnel separated me from the sky, a red glow all around me. It was tall and wide and translucent, and Igloo was on the other side. I never saw him so upset. He cried and clawed at the ground to save me.

He never got the chance.

The ground trembled. Chunks of earth rose into the air. Mountains and crevices formed where there was once flat land. The ground under Igloo split into a deep rift, swallowing him. My eyes tear even as I write this. It is my last memory of the old world, and it is a sad one. There are no dogs allowed in the Dome. But we've all heard them out in the jungle. There will be a day when we find them again.

While the earth shook, the ground swelled and dropped, and I was suspended only by the tunnel's glowing walls. The lake disappeared, and fire shot into the air. But I was safe in the tunnel. Nothing could strike me through those red walls.

I spent many eternities in that tunnel. Either I was moving, or the world was. And then a deafening roar shook my heart, and beyond the tunnel was rushing white water, though it looked pink through the tunnel. Waves. Waves from the ocean.

A group of men found me, carrying swords and supplies. They were the Preceptors of the Dome. One of them picked me up, and another opened my tin and ate the last piece of the cookie. They kept moving through the tunnel, stopping briefly to rest or gather more survivors.

After endless marching, the tunnel ended in the Dome we have now. It spanned miles, a self-enclosed kingdom tinted with that horrible red, but spared from the tremors, eruptions, and floods.

And, of course, the pyramid. Giant stone staircases spanned the four sides, and they ran up to the very top, which disappeared into the heavens in a trail of smoke.

Son, the bell has tolled for this morning's exercises and I must not tarry—

* * *

Finding Home

From *Prophecies of The Great Wu-Shen Kulkulcan*:
Those who eat of my food, and drink of my water, and sleep in my shelter: those are beholden to me with their very lives. Exercise of the mind and body will keep them safe here. Only death will greet them beyond my kingdom.

Ye
6 Etznab 1 Xul

No one blames me for my relationship with Sonja. Other Preceptors have found companionship amongst the Citizens. We're nothing special, she and I. Oh, but if we could prove our fertility, Wu-Shen would treat us like royalty.

It's just a dream, though. Sonja and I have been together for a while, and nothing. Maybe Wu-Shen is right. Maybe we're just not pure enough for children.

Sonja
16 July 2020

I've had to keep this journal hidden for a few days. I made a mistake during Morning Exercises. If there's one thing you need to know, Son, it's never stand out. Not in this place. Do your job just well enough to remain unnoticed.

I was late coming to Exercises. I'd been sneaking around the perimeter of the Dome to pick some of those wild plants—some of the older women teach, in secret, of the plants that can be used as medicine. I found the plant said to help with nausea and chewed it on my way to Exercises. I was late and had to squeeze into the back.

Near all the Preceptors.

I stood next to a man I had never seen before. He was older and had trouble with the exercises. Even with the root, I was trying not to get sick to my stomach, but I noticed the older man started shaking. The Preceptor came right over, ready to report the old man's weakness to Wu-Shen.

Wu-Shen stays in his pyramid and only ever makes an appearance right before Exercises to read us a passage from a book he's written called Prophecies. It's a passage we're supposed to commit to memory and contemplate as we work. But if someone is doing really bad at exercises, they are taken to Wu-Shen himself!

What becomes of them is unspeakable. Sometimes if there's an injury…well, there are surgeons here. They do things like organ transplants. Things that require human donors. Do you understand? The weakest of us are taken for spare parts.

So you understand my concern when I saw this man shaking. The Preceptor approached with chains. It was the only thing I could think to do! I threw up, right there in front of everyone. But it worked. The Preceptors forgot about the old man. Instead, they pulled me aside and examined me. They wanted to quarantine me. I was as good as dead.

I asked the Preceptors to fetch Ye. He talked them out of reporting me to Wu-Shen, and they sent me back to work. By the time I returned, the Citizens were already working on digging a pipeline into the pyramid. I took my place and saw that the man at the end of the line was the same old man I'd seen earlier. I tried not to stare, but his hands trembled.

"Parkinson's," I whispered to him during our lunch break.

"What?"

I was relieved he spoke my language, for I didn't know how to translate the ailment. "You have Parkinson's?" I asked.

He looked grave. "How do you know?"

"My grandfather had it."

The man nodded. He finished his lunch in silence, then turned to me very seriously. I promised him I wouldn't tell. He took my hand. "Thank you for earlier. You saved me. You put yourself at great risk."

I admitted that my lover was a Preceptor. Then I don't know why, but I decided to tell this man about you. About you and my plan to escape. I invited him along.

He frowned. "Why leave?" he asked. "You're in good shape, you have a connection with the Preceptors…it's dangerous out there."

Finding Home

  I put my hand on my belly, and the man nodded solemnly. He understood. "I'm Huang-fu," he said. "If you can think of a way out, I will join you."

* * *

From *Prophecies of The Great Wu-Shen Kulkulcan*:
Sick in body means also sick in spirit. We have not been saved to fester and die infirm. The difficult accomplishments with which we have been tasked do not allow for sickness. He who is infirm in mind or body must remove himself for the greater good. My divine hand will ensure it.

Sonja
21 July 2020
  Huang-fu and I will meet at the boundary after midnight, after the Preceptors have made their rounds. We each have a sword and a canteen, and we will gather what rations we can. Our plan is to escape into the jungle, to find others. To start fresh and provide a place for others who may follow.

  And you, Son. You will be among them. I have some extra blankets for when you arrive. And I've put this off far too long. Your father has no idea…but when Ye comes for me, I will tell him of you. How will he react? Son, if this is my last entry then I wish you luck in this world. I hope you do not grow up in this prison.

  It has been years since they sealed the tunnel, yet Citizens have disappeared. Some went into the pyramid, yes—the sick or the weak. But some of the strongest have disappeared. The Emperor likes to pretend, but I know where they are. We all do.

  There are ways out of the Dome. I have found one of them. I can see what lies beyond the red boundary. It's a lush jungle. The sun has returned. The plants have overgrown everything. Out there, safety is no guarantee—but for the courageous, it'll do. I can't wait to feel the sun against my skin. I will find the others, and we will start over.

  And Son, I will allow my hair to grow.

Ye
4 Muluc 12 Xul
The Great Wu-Shen Kulkulcan has said that he who proves fertile will live in his palace with all its amenities.

I will live like a prince.

Sonja
28 May 2024
Son, I have seen the jungle. I have tasted fresh air. I have felt the sun on my skin. And yet I am back in the Dome, trapped in Kulkulcan's pyramid. It's been nearly four years since our first plan failed, and I have been here ever since, my body festering in this horrible place. But all is not lost, for you are well, and you are somewhere in this same pyramid.

And we have another plan.

It was your father who revealed us. I knew Wu-Shen had too much power over him. I should never have told him about you: Ye refused to escape. He sent the Preceptors after me instead. Old Huang-fu just couldn't keep up in the dense jungle, and I stayed behind to help him. That's how they got me.
Four years ago we were fleeing for our lives in the jungle. I was visibly pregnant, and that's when they caught me. They took us back in chains, both me and Huang-Fu, up to the pyramid. But I haven't time to waste writing of my stupidity, for I have better news to tell. Unfortunately, Ye will not be part of it.

Your father turned us in. He paid his price, though. He was a threat to Wu-Shen, but he is one no longer. He was a good man deep down, though, Son. He was the one who searched me when they brought me to the pyramid. He found this journal, and he kept it safe, returning it to me after Wu-Shen was out of sight. Any other Preceptor would have confiscated it.
Still.

In the short time I had in the jungle, I learned that it's safe to live outside the Dome. The floodwaters have receded, and lush jungle has overgrown the ruined landscape. Fruits and vegetables! Medicines and herbs! My time was cut short, though.

When they took me to the pyramid, they did not take me to be devoured at the base. They kept me in chains as they took me up those never-ending steps. Up-up-up. We entered through an open doorway near the peak, the place where Wu-Shen resides. It was more pleasant than I thought, and I can only hope you live there now: a series of hallways efficiently lit by the sun and designed to harbor the breeze.

Two of the Preceptors took Ye down one of the hallways, and Wu-Shen ordered me to follow down another. He took me to a simple bedroom, lit and ventilated like the hallway. "You are mine now," he said. "Obey me completely and you will want for nothing."

All I could do was nod. He was so powerful, dressed as a feathered serpent, I almost believed him. I think I even bowed.

"He is mine," Wu-Shen said, pointing to my belly. I could still do nothing but nod. "Your servant will arrive shortly." He left without another word.

I stared, dumbfounded, out the window of my room. What a view! I could see the whole lush jungle from there. Of course, it was shrouded in that terrible red glow. Still, I tried to remember the colors of the jungle under the unadulterated deep blue of the sky...

A woman's voice at the door jarred me from my thoughts. I recognized her immediately. Hsing Wen Hsu! My best childhood friend! The one who tried to escape! She wore a drab robe like the rest of us. Her hair was short. Her left leg was missing, though, and she walked with a crutch.

She sat on the bed and whispered to me of her life since I last saw her. She told me of the emperor's attempts to recondition her. No doubt her leg was part of all that. After Hsing Wen's "treatments," the Emperor employed her within his own walls.

But Son, this is what you must understand, for it is part of our plan for you: Hsing Wen's loyalty to the Emperor is only a ploy. In the years she served Wu-Shen Kulkulcan, she learned the secrets that are hidden from the rest of us. Do you see, Son? She is only biding her time.

The most amazing secret she told me is this: Wu-Shen has computers and technology hoarded away, and he refuses to share them with anyone. It's what runs the Dome and keeps us powerless compared to him. It's what makes him a god. Hsing Wen knows where he hides his secret equipment, deep within this very pyramid.

But Son, the light where I am kept now is dark, and I won't waste my time writing of what Hsing Wen can tell you herself. This is my last entry, for I have arranged to send this journal to you this very night. It will be yours to read. Hsing Wen will teach you how. She spoke my language as a child, and she has never forgotten—despite what Wu-Shen Kulkulcan makes us speak. Read, Son! Read of my story, of my past.

Most importantly: heed Hsing Wen's words, for she is now your caregiver. She has Wu-Shen's absolute trust. And she has a following among the pyramid's servants who are ready to start a new life beyond the Dome, beyond Wu-Shen's heavy reach. They are daily finding ways of spreading their message to the Citizens. They are working for a free world. A life in the jungle.

And you will be the crux of their success.

Trust in Hsing Wen as you would trust in me, your own mother. Hsing Wen will raise you, Son, and when the time is right, we will all make our move.

Together.

Hsing Wen will teach you my language, but it is a forbidden tongue—something you must only speak in whispers, and only when no one else is around. But most importantly, make Wu-Shen Kulkulcan think he is to you as a father—for his trust in you is the cornerstone of our plan. Obey him and flatter him. Learn every secret he has to teach.

During my days in the jungle, I found others who are studying medicinal plants. Growing food. Building a town there, hidden in the jungle. I spoke with them enough to learn that there are Preceptors sympathetic to our cause. When you are ready, they will be waiting to help.

But I'm getting ahead of myself.

As for me, I am here in the pyramid with you. Wu-Shen has me locked somewhere in the lower levels. There is little light, and I hear nothing. And once every three days, Wu-Shen descends and comes to me, lusting for a son of his own...

No one is allowed down here in my prison. I am kept in isolation except for a servant who speaks a language I've never heard of. Wu-Shen does this to keep me lonely. After he had your father killed, he claimed you as his own son. I was there in a room at the top of the pyramid, recovering from childbirth, when he announced you as his heir to all those below. He lied to the people. His words echoed in my feverish brain as I lay in pain. He told the people that your mother died in childbirth, that he would raise you on his own, and that you would be his heir.

But in secret, he comes to me. He tries and tries to father his own offspring. Hsing Wen helps with that, too. She found a medicine that protects me from his seed. Sinful as that may be at such a time, I could not bear to carry such spawn.

Wu-Shen has probably already given you a name, just as he once tried to give me one. And you should accept this name and respond to it as your own—accept it in his presence but not in your heart. I want you to know this: Your true name is not what he calls you. The moment I heard your first cry, just before they took you from me, I named you. I named you for my little brother. Your true name, which even Hsing Wen is not allowed to call you within the bounds of the Dome, is Peter. It is what I will call you when first I hold you in my arms someday under the unadulterated blue of the jungle sky...until then, my Peter.

* * *

From *Prophecies of The Great Wu-Shen Kulkulcan*:
Spirit, mind, and body are one; in that order is their strength. The spirit is a fire; the hotter and brighter it burns, the stronger your resolve. The mind, fed by the power of your spirit, controls your body. Your ability to survive, your health, your fertility, your willingness to serve your fellow man, and your desire to do anything you choose to do, rests in the incandescence of your spirit.

Even I, an agent of the divine, cannot change that. I know only that the strength of our own spirits will reap for each of us exactly what we deserve.

A teacher by day and a writer by night, **Val Muller** lives with two corgis and a husband in Northern Virginia. Her short stories range from sci-fi, fantasy, and horror to children's fiction and have appeared in a number of magazines and anthologies. *Corgi Capers*, her first middle-grade mystery novel, will be released soon. You can keep track of her at http://mercuryval.wordpress.com/about.

Forgetfulness

By
Dean Kisling

    I am an anthropologist. I don't mean I was formally trained for the discipline, or that I practice it as a profession. It is only in my nature to be curious about men.

    My livelihood, that is, what I do for money, is working in a bar. I clean tables and toilets and floors, carry things in from the storeroom and out to the dumpster, wash dishes in the small kitchen, and generally perform menial tasks for the bartender, waitress and cook.

    Murphy's Law is a tavern of the working class. Once, that meant journeymen from the construction trades, factory workers and the like—men with callused hands and rough clothes, women with short hair and no loose jewelry. Urban renewal, now grown slightly shabby itself, and offshore manufacturing have changed things over the years. The roughly dressed still come, but they have been joined by others.

    The white-collar workers who come here to drink and eat fried food have risen as far or even a bit beyond their own expectations—or perhaps their expectations have come down to meet them. They seldom speak of advancement, and when they do, the aggravations seem to outweigh the increase in salary, or so they claim. They secretly envy those who work with their hands and sometimes need to be reminded to wash up before they eat. They envy the camaraderie, which they believe is more authentic than what they know in the cubicles. They do not envy the heavy shoes and crooked walks of the plumbers and carpenters and concrete workers and auto mechanics they share the bar with.

They do not recognize that much of the tribal unity of those men is based on uncertain wages, uncertain futures and the aches, pains and deformities caused by work and disappointment. They don't, and yet they do, and that is why they come.

It is no different for them. What we all share in Murphy's Law is the knowledge that things will rarely work out as we imagine.

In the afternoons, the bar is surreal in an ordinary sort of way. We're open, but there are few customers. The staff is mainly getting ready for the evening. The cook lights the griddle around noon and starts serving from the menu at 3:00. Staff can eat around 2:00 for free.

Most of the early customers are the laid off, retired on meager pension, or disabled but still mobile, with empty hours weighing upon them. They are waiting for happy hour, when the gainfully employed start arriving with the comfort of jokes and complaints and curses…and drinks are two for the price of one.

As an amateur anthropologist, I might describe the degree of sadness or happiness as a personality trait in humans. My own observation is that it is not a direct corollary of their life experience. Some of the unfortunate are in a relatively good humor; some of the fortunate are not. I will not suggest I know why or whence this trait, only that it could be plotted as a bell-shaped curve. The "moderately unhappy with occasional moments of happiness" people are grouped at the center of the bell—and from there, twin curves dwindle toward greater extremes of sadness or happiness.

The patrons of Murphy's Law are, I would say, on the whole, toward the middle but on the low side. I would not say this to anyone's face, however. I have to work here.

Finding Home

It was just called Murphy's when I began working here many years ago. Ownership has changed several times. During the brighter days of shifting demographics the name was changed to Murphy's Law. I presume *that* owner, whom I only briefly met, imagined the facetiously witty and rebellious name would attract the more educated, more upwardly mobile, more recently arrived denizens of the neighborhood.

The older, shorter name is still used, but it is accepted custom that one must pass through an initiation period and gain the status of a regular before using it, or risk receiving contemptuous glances. Certainly, there are territorial issues involved, but the primary factor seems to be the capacity to be properly socialized within Murphy's environment. New arrivals, whether staff or customer, are observed and measured by some unspoken and elusive standards before they are accepted. There was considerable tension when the white-collar class of workers first started patronizing the bar. But that tension has resolved into something resembling the banter and friendly insults traded by fans of rival sports teams.

I myself have achieved acceptance by a combination of appearing defective in a more or less unthreatening way, and being worn but economically serviceable. Like the furnishings and mechanisms, the tables and chairs, the cooler and grill, the scarred bar itself, with its reupholstered stools and dented brass foot-rail, I have been passed along and enjoy a humble, semi-respectable position. I am like the older memorabilia on the walls.

No one knows exactly how I came to be here or why, but it is taken for granted there must be some reason. I might be someone's relative. My wages might be subsidized by some non-profit organization or government program. I might be the modern day village idiot, the lucky one, upon whom some pity has been taken, because I can adequately perform simple tasks and do not suffer problematic episodes of behavior.

These are not unreasonable speculations. I am short and have vaguely mongoloid features. I have learned to be restrained and cautious in my speech. Newcomers to Murphy's are often nervously uncertain about me. Those who display fearful or aggressive attitudes toward me are soon chastized by the regulars.

They are told in no uncertain terms: "Freddy is all right, leave Freddy alone."

I appreciate this support, and of course I take some advantage of it too. On occasion, I deliberately say something knowledgeable, intelligent or deviously comic, just to disconcert their assumptions. People mess with me, I mess with them back. I have mystique on my side after all.

As one long-time customer put it, "everybody sticks out their elbows, their thorns, their bad smell or bad temper, whatever they've got, just trying to make a little room for themselves in a crowded place."

Then another guy said "bad haircut."

And another said, "bad mojo," and another said "bad suit," and around, people said "bad breath," and "bad genes," and "bad influences." And people laughed and it made me feel among brothers—standing there with my broom like the sorcerer's apprentice—and for hours after you would still hear someone say that's some bad mojo man, or like a bad suit bro, or some other bad thing and laugh again. Say what you might—excuse me—say what I might about the fickleness of the tribe—you gotta love these guys.

As far as I know, I am now the longest habitant of Murphy's present. There was an old guy—he was an old guy when I met him—and he used to still come by from time to time, and then once or twice with a younger companion. I haven't seen him for a while though, and I don't really expect to. He didn't look well. He said something about having a drink before he went to that big union hall in the sky.

What I mean is…my right to be here is not seriously disputed. My cover is not blown. I have been cashing my paychecks with the same guy for so long he only charges me five percent now. I'm not telling you where I live, for reasons I think will become clear, but I have lived there since my early days at Murphy's, paying my rent in cash from my typical minimum wage plus tips plus food. I don't think I could survive without the tips and food, but they have always been there.

Finding Home

The bartender and the waitress divide up the tips for the night and share with the cook and me. The method of cash distribution is changeable, dependent on mood and need and how much or little cash is there, and other things: sadness and happiness. It is not known to me exactly how they decide. Possibly, they have a telepathic discussion of the matter out of my range.

When I say I was not formally trained, I do not mean to imply I have not studied. I have little money for books, of course, but I have a library card. Lacking any social life other than the bar and riding the bus, I have plenty of free time. I have always had a facility with language. That was a gift and I take no credit for it, but I have done my best to use it to good purpose.

The librarians have been very helpful. Among other things, they taught me how to use the Internet, after the computers were installed. Between the books, the bar and the World Wide Web, I can encounter nearly every idea, opinion, discovery and falsehood ever disseminated by human beings. That can be rather overwhelming at times, but in the long run it has given me an appreciation for the simplicity underlying so many things that seem complex. For instance, just in terms of remaining alive, you are either hungry or nourished, and people may treat you well or badly.

Then too, the TV is always on at Murphy's. News, athletic contests, science, history, movies and propaganda flow from the screen all of my working hours. The drama of TV and the bar patrons' reactions to it has played a large role in my understanding of life on earth and what matters most to the people who live here.

That's where I first heard about the faster than light experiment, on the TV. It was briefly mentioned on an afternoon science program. I was intrigued, and later I looked it up on the Internet in the library.

An energy signal was transmitted across some kind of highly excited, supercharged plasma medium to a receiver on the other side. It went across the gap at 300 times the speed of light. It arrived before it left.

The scientists declared their experiment cast no doubt on relativity theory. The energy signal arrived without meaningful order in it, no information, no message. They weren't sure you could even say anything had actually *happened*, only that it had happened very fast. Einstein's theory of the constant but relative speed of light was about the orderly movement of information through time and space. The experiment proved Einstein correct, they said, because it demonstrated that at faster than light speed, information would be lost.

I was interested in the experiment because I had already figured that out on my own.

This came up today because of a guy named Dave. Dave is a mechanical engineer who designs heating and cooling systems for buildings. Dave likes to talk about the end of the world. He's full of stories about Nostradamus and the Bible Code and the Mayans and Hindus and Egyptians and astronomy and corporate cartels and Big Brother and ice ages and electromagnetic flares from the sun and other scenarios for the end of days. He's quite well versed in these subjects. He has tracked various conspiracy theories and a string of disappointing predictions regarding the actual date of doom. He is sure we are in the end times now, though. He says it's like mankind is moving into another dark age by mutual and strange attraction. We're going there because we can.

Lately, Dave has become rather more political in his description of the modern world—but he is putting his real hopes on aliens from space. And because that is part of Mayan lore, he is wondering about the Mayan calendar and 2012 and all that. His argument is that between the astronomy, biology, anthropology, quantum theory, Mayans, and other stuff, you can make a reasonable case for alien visitation or seeding—and interstellar space travel (never mind intergalactic travel) is really not conceivable without faster than light speed, and the more faster the better. Dave's current vision is basically *1984* with benevolent and powerful visitors from space at the end.

So it was Dave who actually started the conversation about this faster than light experiment. He says other faster than light experiments were done in the twentieth century, but none anywhere near as fast as this one. Scientists don't know what to make of them, really. It's not good enough to just say it doesn't violate relativity theory; it's not supposed to be possible, but there it is.

It raised some interesting questions. If you traveled faster than light would you go into the past? Could you have an effect there? Would all information be lost, or only some of it—maybe only the part that organized the rest into a coherent narrative of universal events? And what did it mean to arrive before you left? It gradually becomes clear that what Dave pictures: earth's descendants traveling among the stars. They will return in time to guide us and save us from ourselves. And if the Mayan calendar is right, we don't have long to wait now. He likes 2012 because it's not too far away and he'll probably live to see it. Or live to regret it, quips someone down the bar.

Dave's concept of proper aliens from space is humanoid creatures who have entirely gotten over being self-destructive and mean to others. Just how this quality might be transferred to contemporary humans is part of the mystery. He says the aliens would have technology and knowledge we can't even imagine. It would be like trying to explain television to someone in the sixth century. The aliens would be firm but patient. They would set a good example. They would not try to capitalize on their celebrity and make space sluts of themselves. They would give more than they took… perhaps that, in itself, would be such a novel experience for humanity it would cause a cognitive dissonance that led to an evolutionary shift in consciousness. He says he is kidding, but maybe not.

"Benevolent visitor from outer space action figures," says someone.

Dave ignores some of the most intriguing evidence, however. What of all the mysterious sightings and maneuvers and abductions and other weird stuff? Granted, the often-anecdotal and uncertain nature of this evidence—but does this sound like the behavior of vastly evolved and benevolent visitors from a superior civilization? Or does it sound like teenage boys and ritualized vandalism? Showing off and marking their territory.

Setting something on fire, or spray-painting the side of a building. Initiations and pranks. Lights in the sky, crop circles, anal probes—they aren't revealing much in the way of wisdom or technology. Is it an "Aliens: Coming Soon" promotional campaign? A galactic youth gang tagging their turf? Space cadets gone wild? How did they get the keys to the spaceship? Do their probation officers know where they are and what they're doing?

I suppose an entirely different wave of visitors might show up at the last minute in 2012. I wouldn't know about that. I came with the earlier wave and I know Dave's hopes about us are not going to pan out, and I know why. It's that faster than the speed of light problem, the loss of information.

We assumed we had embarked with a mission. You see, we had hopes for ourselves too. Faster than light travel made us forget so very many things. Here we were in this spacecraft and we didn't know why, and we had technology onboard we didn't know what it was or how to use it. (I still think the anal probe was actually meant for some other use.) But we had our native intelligence, and an inspiring certainty in our purpose—if only we could remember what it was. We were sure it had something to do with men. We felt strongly about that. I feel strongly about it to this day.

It's all very *Lord of the Flies* meets *X Files*. But as far as wise-men-from-the-stars-coming-to-save-humanity goes… it's not looking real good. I know what I'm talking about. I think it's just a hobby for Dave, but it's a somewhat optimistic one, and well suited to his interests, and I wouldn't want to spoil it for him even if I dared to speak up, which I don't.

I jumped ship, if you want to know. We got earth TV on the ship, and apparently I retained a natural talent for language and logic. I watched and listened to human beings telling the story of themselves. The cop shows, especially, demonstrated their longing for kindness and justice.

I came to the conclusion that humans, despite their confused blend of arrogance and fear, were in fact trying to become better than they were. I thought they deserved better treatment than we were giving them.

I was not successful at convincing my companions of this. If I were to apply human psychology to them, I would say my shipmates had become psychotic. And I would guess that was due to the loss of their own history, their lack of connection and sense of belonging to something greater than themselves.

Since I failed utterly in my attempts to reason with them, I just decided to take my chances on the ground. I admit this was not an entirely altruistic decision based on empathy for earthlings. My own personal sense of shame simply became intolerable.

My old posse is still doing pretty much the same as they did years ago, except they don't do livestock mutilations much anymore. I regret that I had to abandon them, but what else could I do in such circumstances? Now *they* are on TV: "Invasion of the Clueless from Outer Space."

It is possible, of course, that I am a future descendant of earth, that I have traveled faster than light, and backward in time, and therefore information has been lost. This could be interpreted from an optimistic perspective, even if it does not quite match Dave's vision. Humanity must have survived somehow, moved on and even tried to come back and make things better at a particularly crucial moment. We look kind of alike and have many things in common—including lots of technology but less than a full lick of common sense.

The speed of light limit exists to maintain an orderly evolution throughout the universe—to allow the universe to listen to itself and learn what it is doing. No short cuts are allowed. Short cuts produce chaos, weird feedback loops that make the message incoherent. We all just do the best we can with what we've got in the time we have.

That's how it works at Murphy's. I'm sure that's why I fit in so well. Like my brothers at the bar, I am lost but somehow right at home. Lonely, but not alone.

Dean Kisling

Dean Kisling is a high school dropout who learned to type when he was 47. He has been a soldier, laborer, driver, welder, carpenter, musician, trailrunner and fool. He is a little worn out and beat up from those adventures, but has retained a sense of humor and a sense of hope about human existence. His short stories have been published around the internet in ezines, ebooks, audio and video. He writes stories about what happened and also makes stuff up. He is very pleased to be in this anthology of stories imagining a hopeful future. He lives in America and is very happily married. His website is http://pneumerology.com

Part III
Rule Makers & Breakers

Consensus

By
Timons Esaias

      George heard humming echo through the tunnel, Bethuna's humming, and tried not to visibly flinch. Ted and his son Tad, who lived higher up the Juniata ridge, made room in the bench-niche, and the teenager instinctively stowed away the laptop he'd been playing with. Nobody liked to be caught playing when Bethuna came to visit.

      That bench on which they sat, carved out of the side of this passage, had been George's best inspiration yet, and people were copying it all over the township. It was nice to make tunneling into a social activity. He could chip away at the tunnel face, or side niches, and folks could visit and chat. When the tunnel advanced and the bench got too far from the working area, he'd just cut another and use the old niche for a cupboard space.

      He had a brief memory-flash of colleagues gathering around a fireplace, at a ski lodge, back before deliberate combustion had been outlawed. Best not to dwell on that. He set his chisel again, and tapped it a few times to let Bethuna know where he might be found, and that he was working, so that she couldn't came across as all morally superior.

Bethuna liked to make her rounds when she would find people at ease, rather than at work. I'm working, her body language would say, and you're not, so my way is right.

The fiber-optic cable shed enough light into this tunnel for her to see the open space on the bench, but Bethuna ignored it, and sank to her haunches instead. Benches are decadent, her posture said. Benches are the old way, and you lose too much body heat to the rock.

They exchanged greetings, and George kept chipping, scoring the outline of an eye-level shelf. He liked to make his passages narrow, both to reduce labor and to keep the structure of the rock intact. The consensus agreement on how much space could be carved out of a given volume struck him as far too generous, and he preferred to make niches rather than storage rooms. Even his pantry was a series of narrow aisles slotted off a hallway, with niche shelves, rather than an open room with plastic or wooden shelving. Bethuna had made some public noises about that, suggesting it was too labor intensive, but people seemed to think it was his business and not theirs. She had ultimately let the issue drop.

It was clear to George that Ted wanted to deny her the satisfaction of being asked her business. Instead, he asked her how things were going with the greenhouse design. George knew that Ted resented the fact that Bethuna spent her days working down in the valley at the hospital, and that all her family either worked there too, or were permanent patients. The hospital was the only building in the township fully above ground, the only building kept at 65° in winter instead of the 56° that the caves offered, the only building that wouldn't invite a United Commonwealths IR-seeking missile if it generated excess heat. The only building that was dehumidified.

What galled Ted especially, as he'd said to George many times, was the way she came up from the hospital and spent the evenings telling other people what they had to do without; why it was they couldn't work in the hospital; why their people weren't sick enough or old enough to be admitted there; and 'oh, by the way,' why whatever it is they liked most needed to be examined for utility or heat budget or some such.

George couldn't help but feel the same way. On the other hand, he wouldn't want her job. The woman was a pain, and he loathed her humming, loathed her constant implied superiority, loathed her whipcord lean body that seemed to need only half the calories that anybody else's did. He loathed the way she sucked dry black-eyed peas in her cheek, as she was doing right then, in an ongoing reproach of people who used fresh water to soak legumes, and solar cookers to cook them. The woman hadn't had cooked food in a decade, and she let everybody know it. Part of her unending quest to let everybody know she lived more lightly on the land than they could. Still, she *had* undertaken the job of consensus manager, which no one else wanted. And she certainly put in the time—even if the main unspoken consensus in the township was that everyone wished she would manage a lot less consensus.

It didn't surprise him that the first sentence of her reply threatened the whole project. "Well, some people have some doubts about what a greenhouse structure does to our heat budget. Maybe it needs to be offset with mirrors or something."

"I thought that issue had been dealt with," George said, keeping his voice soft, just to let her know she was out of line. "The U.C. reference numbers on solar retention systems were studied quite carefully. If people want more mirrors, they can do that on their own consensus."

Bethuna didn't say anything to that, and George's heart sank. Such restraint on her part could only mean that she was holding a better card, something that would get him back.

Ted looked like he had the same idea, and George guessed immediately what he was thinking. Somebody wanted to screw with the glass foundry, Ted's crowning achievement. He'd created a grinding mill that turned the sandstone rubble people were chipping out of the ridge into a powder, using only the power of a small stream that formed whenever it rained. Then he had constructed a solar furnace that turned the powder into molten glass and poured that out into sheets. All with a simple set of controls that a ten-year-old could manage. He had won dozens of citations when the design went on the Net, and provided an alternative to salvaging glass from abandoned surface buildings. Ted's neighbors had then pushed for greenhouses that would attach to the underground chambers that were more and more a part of people's lives. By circulating the air it was hoped they might live a bit more warmly, without wasting the condensation that formed on the walls; the humid, mold-growing condensation that made so many of them miserable with allergies.

"What I'm here about," she said, unable to hold back the bad news any longer, "is the methane budget."

I should quit trying to be nice, George thought. This woman is really evil. It isn't just that she revels in the job nobody else wanted. No, she resented Ted's success, and she had to hit back. Had to undermine everything. Wouldn't let the least improvement of living conditions or morale go unpunished. He almost said it, but didn't want to fight this woman. He hated fights, hated unpleasantness. He just wanted to tend his plants, improve the caves, and manage his compost system. That's what she meant to attack, his composting. Half the point of the greenhouses would be lost if they couldn't keep the soil rich through compost.

He kept his tongue locked up, and Ted wouldn't respond either.

It was Tad who finally gave her a reply. "You can have mine," he said.

It was the only opening she was going to get, so she took it. "It isn't going to be enough to eliminate all but the most vital combustion," she said, pointedly ignoring what Tad had said, "even though waste heat is the major culprit in global warming. The people who know are saying that we need to scrub out any greenhouse gases we can, and generate as few as we must. Now, it's true that composting has been seen as a virtue for many years, and it's natural and organic and all that. But it's the biggest methane generator outside of mammalian intestines."

"Sure—" Tad started, but Bethuna talked right over him.

"It was all very well when we could burn the methane for fuel, but those days are gone. There's a consensus proposal that we either find a way to use the methane without combustion, or stop composting altogether."

Ted asked her if anybody had figured out what they were going to do with all their sewage if they couldn't compost it, but George wasn't really listening to the answer. The answer would be negative, some form of "Not really" hidden by Bethuna's bossy language. That's the way she always works, he thought. She always wants to stop something and she always pretends it's some kind of progressive challenge.

"Is this a township proposal, or more general?" George asked.

She took another black-eyed pea out of her scrip and looked at it, rather than at him. George became self-conscious about the fact that he wasn't trying to meet her eyes, either, but had been watching her sidelong and pretending to concentrate on his tools. "This is a bottom-up action right now," Bethuna said, "but it's coming up all over the world."

Which George interpreted to mean that she had seen it somewhere and turned the idea to her own purposes. For the good of the planet, of course, and the rapid defeat of global overheating.

Ted started to argue, quietly, with Bethuna, but George only half listened. He tried to line up his chisel again, but his heart wasn't in that either. Instead he found himself wondering at just what point life would become intolerable for him, and how soon that moment would arrive. He had been a journalist, making a nice living, but the ban on paper production and the restriction of Net usage had taken that away. Journalists could still contribute, and he did, but it no longer earned money or anything tradable. Now he was a gardener, and the organic waste manager for half the Juniata side of the ridge. Or he would be until Bethuna changed it into something he wouldn't be willing to do any more, by means of this new "consensus."

His other passion in life had been the oracles of the earth. He had taken two months off work every year to live near an ancient site like Dodona, Cumae, Epidaurus or Borobudur, soaking in the atmosphere, learning the modern language of the place, and wondering at the vastness of time and the imagination. His books on Ephesus and Siwa had both won awards.

He would never see such places again, of course. There were no airplanes or liners or even freighters or tankers to take across the ocean. Sailing ships now plied the seas, and it cost a fortune to sign up as an untrained deckhand. A fortune he didn't have, and never would. Accumulated wealth was dangerous, and the world no longer allowed it.

His thoughts then went to a technical question he'd been daydreaming about during his last few shifts with the compost piles. At what point would civilization actually be officially, technically broken down? While it was true that there was little in the way of warfare anymore, and a form of world government existed, and a fairly universal Net… it was also true that ground was being lost every day. Medical research wasn't keeping up, and almost everything else humans were doing involved adapting to the displacements caused by the rising oceans, abandoned coastal cities, warming climate and the cessation of all deliberate combustion.

The adaptation had been amazing. Truly amazing. But George doubted that civilization would be sustained for very long in self-denial mode. George met everyone in his job, because everyone generated organic waste. His sense was that the people in this township were hanging on, but losing heart, just as he felt himself doing this very moment. There were no victories in their days, just deferred disasters.

He set the chisel bit in the groove again, tapped it with the maul twice, and wondered again how much he could take before he lost heart himself; before he decided that this life was no longer worth living. That he should quit breathing and making carbon dioxide, waste heat, and methane.

He moved the chisel, tapped twice more, tasted the saltiness of the stone that had been laid down when Pennsylvania was on the seabed, and realized it had just happened. Right then. This woman, Bethuna, who was that moment snarling something about the sins of their fathers forcing the present discomforts on their sons—and pointedly not using gender-neutral language—

this woman was guiding the township to despair through self-hatred and self-denial.

"My father…" George said, interrupting what the others were saying. They paused because he was their host. "My father worked for the phone company, but he thought of himself as an inventor. Bought all sorts of gizmos, and turned our garage into this bizarre workshop. My mother was always screaming in the winter that the car would never start because it sat out in the freezing cold, while a perfectly good garage went to waste right in front of it.

"She was right about the waste. Dad loved engineering, but he didn't really have a clue. I expect he was insane, but kept the insanity boxed up in that garage. If you asked him what his latest invention was supposed to do, he'd give you exact details. Ask him *how* it would do it, he got mysterious and vague. Didn't want to give away his secrets before his patents came in, that kind of thing. At first I kind of suspected that he wasn't sure what he was doing, and then I was certain of it. He couldn't drive me to college when I left home, because he had to finish the drawings of his All-Weather Radiation Re-delineator. The thing was huge. Stood about twelve feet high and must have been twenty-five feet long. It poked out the garage door and that end had to be covered with a tarp to keep prying eyes away. I think the floor was cracking under the weight. The last time I saw him alive he was admiring his work."

George paused, not entirely sure what had brought that story to mind. Maybe he was feeling clueless himself? Or that all his efforts in life were wasted?

"What did it do?" Tad asked.

"Nothing, I'm sure. But it was *supposed* to take infrared radiation and turn it into ultra-violet radiation and shoot it off into space. All while breaking carbon dioxide down and making more oxygen. Just put it out in the sun, he said, and it would cool the planet and give the forests something to breathe."

Tad tilted his head. "But forests breathe carbon dioxide, not oxygen."

"Yeah," George said. "Dad had trouble getting his facts straight." George lined up the point of his chisel again, tapped it with the maul, blew the dust out of the groove and hit it again. I have given up on my old life, he thought. I will no longer live it.

"How sad," Bethuna said.

"At least he was trying," George said, as quietly as he could manage. George intended to speak quietly, and carefully, and respectfully, from here on out. He put down the chisel, then methodically rolled all the tools into an oil-soaked chamois. This shelf would be a long time finishing.

Ted must have decided that George had finished, and he began arguing about the methane budget again. He was not going to agree that composting should be stopped "until a clearly superior alternative was proposed and somebody agreed to do the work" whatever it might be.

George sat down in the empty space between Tad and Ted, while Bethuna and Ted traded nastiness disguised as political discussion. He let his head rest against the cool, damp wall, and felt the little vibrations that traveled through the rock from the hundreds of other rooms inhabited by his neighbors. He could probably hear some tiny echo of every human life on the planet, he realized. The sea has risen, but the bedrock still connects us.

"Well," she was saying, as she always did, "if you want my job, you can just have it." Her voice dripped martyrdom, and that little touch of self-satisfaction that came with having spoiled someone's quiet evening. It would not matter to her if no consensus came to stop the composting. She had put the thing on the table, and she could revisit it again in six months, a year, another year.

"Okay," George said. He needed a new life. "That's what I'll do. I'll take your job."

He would begin with consensus.

Timons Esaias

Timons Esaias is a satirist, poet and writer of short fiction, living in Pittsburgh. His work has appeared in fifteen languages. He won an Asimov's Readers Award; and was a finalist for the British Science Fiction Award. He has had over a hundred poems in print, including Spanish, Swedish and Chinese translations, in markets ranging from *Asimov's Science Fiction* to *5AM* and *Elysian Fields Quarterly: The Literary Journal of Baseball*. His poetry chapbook, *The Influence of Pigeons on Architecture*, sold out two editions. *News Nots*, a faux news column, confused readers of seven different papers, as well as an online audience, for a decade. Chess, historical wargames, aikido, and square-foot vegetable gardening are his chief hobbies. He is Adjunct Faculty at Seton Hill University, in the Writing Popular Fiction M.F.A. Program; and students fear him. He tends to go on and on about stuff.

Maps as Currency

By
Melissa Dominic

I. Nate

     Nate remembered the sound of children.
     It was one of the only things he remembered. Catcalls and tiny, lifted voices screaming something he couldn't understand. They surrounded him when he couldn't hear. His body had felt dank and heavy, humid like the skies and falling fast against the pavement. He remembered lying down, face to the road, a certain shade of black settling in.
     He must have passed out.
     When Nate came to, he was in a bedroom, lying on a mattress on the floor. He had no idea where he was or how he had gotten there. All he could do was guess.
     The people of the Quarantine Nation, the children of the once sick and dying, populated the Eastern American Outlands. These were children who survived, who didn't contract second and third-rate versions of the virus that wiped their parents' generations out. The only people left after a civil war that wrecked the entire United States.

These Quarantine children were locked out of many places and they grew up scattered around the Outlands, making do with what they could find, traveling far and long. Nate assumed these were the people who had picked him up. The same sort of people who had thrown him out of their encampments and tiny towns for asking too many questions, for trying to rally them to travel. Quarantine children were peculiar sorts, and they didn't like his type: a western kid who traveled with purpose, who traveled more than to survive.

Lying on the mattress, clutching his backpack, Nate wondered what his saviors would say about him.

It wasn't long before he heard them.

I. The House of the Silent Skyline

A girl came first.

She had blue eyes that looked like sapphires he had seen simulated in textbooks, and her dark hair was razor cut, accenting the sharp lines of her cheekbones and her chin. She wore layers of skirts and tank tops, scarves and shawls that dragged pieces of fabric on the floor in a pattern of how she walked.

Her smile was slight, perked up only at the edges.

"What's your name?" She asked Nate. Her voice was more gravelly than he expected. She produced an apple from one of the pockets of her skirt. It was small with dull, yellow skin. She held it out to him, her head cocked in offering.

He hesitated, instead pulling his knees further under his chin. The room spun, the edges still dark. There wasn't much around him, just a mattress on the ground and a window bolted shut.

The girl sat on the edge of a low dresser, holding the apple in her lap. When he said nothing, she spoke again. "My name is Ithica." She held the apple up. "And, you should really eat something. You don't look very good." She offered it out, her eyebrow raised slightly.

"I'm Nathaniel," he said, taking the fruit. It felt unnatural in his hand, but it was firm. Fresh.

"Nathaniel..." Her voice trailed. "It's nice to meet you."

She stood, her hands lost in the deep brown and beige swirls, tulle and frayed cotton, of her skirt. Under it all she had on a pair of wrapped up black boots, the heels and edges worn down. Not knowing what to do, Nate held the apple back out to her and smiled.

"It's nice to meet you, too," he said.

Ithica looked at him curiously before she took the apple. Smiling, she took a bite before passing it back.

"You gave us quite a scare out there." Her dark lashes were heavy as she blinked. "We don't take well to running the half-dead over in the streets."

"I'd guess it happens a lot out here." Nate said through bites of the apple.

"More than you'd like to know."

Ithica pulled up one of the edges of her skirts and started for the door. She leaned against the old, worn out wood and knocked twice before looking back at him.

"Don't mind the others."

"There are others?"

"Yeah, and they're all not as kind as me."

Nate went to speak, but she turned again, knocking hard at the door. He heard a click on the other side of the frame and the door swung open. She slipped through as it closed. Nate jumped quickly to his feet and jiggled the handle, but it did nothing. It remained shut. The apple slipped out of his hands and onto the floor, picking up the dust of unswept floorboards.

That was when he realized he had been locked in.

II. Nate

There wasn't much to Nate. He was a mapmaker and he was small and slight with light brown hair cut ragged with a sharp knife. He was a seventeen year old with a map inherited from a dead father and a backpack laced with charms to store it in. Those were the things he counted on. Nothing more, nothing else.

Nate was a boy on an adventure to map the places he had never been and the things he had never seen. Ever since childhood, he had stolen slices of paper and old napkins to make crude line drawings of places he had been to. It was what he did.

Before his father's death, he had been planning the biggest trip for them. They would finally settle down, find a home and live the life they both had wanted, a life with a home and a garden, friends and a family that would grow and grow and grow. People he could know and places he could see. A school, a job, a future.

With his father gone and his journey laid out ahead of him in small steps, Nate did only what was natural. He began to follow the path. He would finish the trip on his own. There was no other choice. He had nothing else left. The map of a place called The Standing City was his father's key, the focus of the cross-country trek.

He kept the map locked up. He wouldn't show it to anyone. He wouldn't let them try and take away his future.

II. The House of the Silent Skyline

The doctor came in after Ithica left. He was tall, thick, and broad shouldered with glasses and messy brown hair he kept pulled back into a ponytail. From behind his ear he pulled a pen and from his pocket, a notepad, where he made a few scratchings before even looking up.

"I'm locked up in here, aren't I?" Nate asked. He looked at the doctor with narrow eyes. The silence unnerved Nate. "There's no one with me you could ask for ransom…" Nate tensed his body, even though it still felt weak. Sunburn ached on the backs of his arms, the hollows of his neck. The doctor reached out, and Nate flinched.

"We're mostly worried you might be sick," the doctor said, holding his hands up. He pushed the glasses up his face and the meager light highlighted the baby-roundness of his face. He looked young. Younger than most doctors Nate had ever encountered. It made him uneasy. The doctor took a step closer, holding out his hand again. Nate sat still, staring up at him.

"Ithica didn't seem too worried."

"She's like that," the doctor said quietly, "always wanting to meet the new kid in town." He paused a moment, giving a sigh. "Would it be alright if I checked you, at least? Let me prove her right. I don't think you want to stay in here all night, do you?"

Nate thought about it for a moment. It felt like a scene in the shows his father would try and patch through into on the pirate television stations. Good cops, bad cops. He was worried about what was next. In a tentative motion, he offered out his wrist, though, and stuck out his tongue.

The doctor gave a little laugh. "You know what they say about strangers when they come to town?" He said as he took notes after peering into Nate's eyes.

"No…"

"They always come with an offer you can't refuse."

"I don't have…" Nate began before the door swung open again and a tall boy with the same blue eyes as Ithica came in. He was tall, with a sort of stare that ignored Nate and bore straight into the back of the doctor's neck.

"He sick, Mathias?"

The doctor sighed. "No, he seems fine." He began to pack away his things.

"Good. I heard your girlfriend was sharing food with him. At least you know now you aren't infected." The boy looked from Mathias to Nate and winked.

Mathias just scowled. "She's your sister, James, show some respect," he said, before letting himself out, locking the pair in once again.

James stayed behind and folded himself cross-legged on the floor next to Nate's makeshift bed. He waited a moment before saying anything, concentrating instead on picking at the frayed sheet edges that hung off the mattress and onto the ground.

"Where are you from?" James finally asked. His limbs were skinny, jeans tailor fit to his legs. His clothing seemed to be the boyish version of Ithica's, in angled cuts and flowing sections.

"The West," Nate said.

James let out a low whistle.

"Quarantine zone?"

"No."

"But you like to travel in them?" James asked.

"Sometimes."

James quirked his head to the side, examining Nate.

Nate shifted under the scrutiny, shaking his head so milk brown hair covered his eyes.

Nate had never been sick, never had close contact with any disease before his father passed away. Being checked and prodded, it all felt wrong to him. People being scared of him threw him off.

He was better at being scared of them instead. In the past, they had always been the ones to let him down. He had long since decided it would be just him.

"Dinner is in an hour," James said suddenly, standing up. He dusted off his jeans and cracked his neck. "I expect you have a timepiece?"

"I have three, actually." Nate blinked. He brushed the hair away from his eyes as quick as he had let it slip there, catching James's gaze and the small smile that played on his lips.

"Good. Don't be late."

* * *

Nate arrived five minutes before the hour was up at an aging wooden table in what seemed to be an old country kitchen. There were curtains pulled over the windows and dishes drying beside the sink.

Ithica, Mathias and James were seated and four bowls of stew steamed. Everything was mismatched in chipped porcelain dishes and mugs with missing handles. Yet, everything was clean. It seemed like home.

Something about it made him smile. The feelings of being trapped in the room bleed away from him. He felt his shoulders relax, his neck ease. They didn't want to capture him. He wasn't a prisoner. They were worried and scared, just like him.

"You're late." James smirked. "I thought you had a time piece."

"The battery must be slow." Nate returned.

James's grin grew.

"Who cooked?" Nate changed the subject.

"I did," Mathias said, "but Ithica helped."

Nate nodded. "It looks good."

"It is," James said glancing over to the empty chair. It was obvious they weren't going to begin without him.

Nate, self-conscious for a moment, slipped over and pulled his chair out. Everyone's spoons dug in the moment Nate's chair squeaked into place. He took a spoonful, closing his eyes.

"Is it good?" Mathias asked.

"Extremely."

The stew was thick with what tasted like root vegetables and seasonings. Heavy spice to mask to mask the taste if things had gone past ripe.

Nate looked from Ithica to Mathias to James before settling his gaze. Each one stared back, perched uncomfortably in their seats.

"So, stranger," James smiled, "what brings you with us today? Where were you going when we found you?"

Nate flinched. "Nowhere, I was just sort of…" He started, but quickly stopped. There was no use lying to himself, or to them. He knew he had been going somewhere before he stopped. He knew exactly where he had been going. He looked down at his bowl of food, the steam wafting up and filling him with a sense of home, a sense of camaraderie. He sighed deeply.

"What do you know of the Standing City? I was going to the Standing City…" he said

All three sets of eyes stared back. They said nothing.

"Do you think you can help me get there?"

James spoke first. His voice delicate and fine, teetering on the edge of broken glass. "Once you leave the Standing City," he said, "you can't really go back."

"And all three of us have already left." Ithica finished for him.

Mathias was the one to look away.

Nate chewed on his lip. He focused hard to keep his eyes from going wide. "So you've all been there. You know where it is? You can help me then?"

"It's not that easy, Nate." Ithica whispered. She pushed aside her dinner and let her spoon fall on the table with a clank.

"What do you mean it's not that easy? Are we near it? Where am I now? I have no idea. I've been trying to get to it for so long. No one'll help me. No one. You guys too? I've never met anyone who has been there and now…now?" Nate forgot all about his dinner to pull out a small, beat-up journal. He turned to a map and fiddled with a pencil he found in the other pocket.

He looked up at them expectantly.

Again they just stared at him.

His shoulders slumped. His pencil made a baseless line on the page. "At least tell me where I am…"

"You're in the Black City," Mathias answered. "Largest quarantine city just outside of the Standing City. And by 'large' we mean more than ten people live here."

"There are points high enough where you can see the walls of Standing City," Ithica offered, "but that's all. No way to see inside."

"I don't need to see inside," Nate bristled, "I have a map."

"A map?" James questioned. "What sort of map?"

"A map to the inside of the Standing City."

Mathias let out a low whistle and Ithica turned to her brother.

James, stoic, stared Nate down. "Well, kid," he said, digging into his stew for another mouthful. He chewed and swallowed. "That changes everything."

III. Nate

Nate often found himself pulling the map out late at night, memorizing the streets and alleyways of the city he had never seen. The city that survived the end of the world.

A city he wasn't allowed inside.

His father had never taken *No* for an answer and Nate had decided he would stop. He would keep on going, keep on staring, keep on memorizing even when he was told it was impossible, that it would never happen.

It had consumed him.

One thing Nate loved about the map was it meant that someone lovingly put the time into charting out their surroundings. It meant that the lines and the calculations were populated by people, living, breathing people who formed unions, who made enemies, who lived together, in close contact.

Nate had been traveling so long he had forgotten what that was like. It was something he wanted back badly.

III. The House of the Silent Skyline

"I'll take him for a walk," Ithica said.

Nate realized James could jump over the kitchen table and strangle him for not saying anything sooner. He quickly agreed to the walk.

"I like it out here," she said, once they were far enough away. Their kitchen belonged to a family that had died years before, like most of the families in the Black City, and became abandoned, like most of the homes in the Black City.

Both of them had a flashlight in their pocket, and Ithica held a large pot of leftovers in two hands. The sun hadn't gone down yet, but Ithica told him it would and the city would live up to its name.

"It isn't bad," Nate said, glancing around as the streets became slightly more dilapidated, the trees cut down or broken and left unclean. "If you find a way to make it habitable, I'm sure—where is the food going, though?"

"Mathias's family lives around here. They could always use extra food." Ithica wiggled the pot slightly. "They think I cook it and Mathias thinks they don't need to know that I only help."

"Everyone around here is a family," Nate said in a low whisper.

"Wait until we reach Central Street."

The walk didn't take long, and Ithica wouldn't let Nate wrangle the pot from her hands. She kept telling him just to watch the streets, to be careful, to pay attention, clucking at him like he was her little brother.

So he did, and when Central Street came into view, Nate didn't have to look up at the street sign, he could tell by the strands of children playing in the street and the older men and women playing dominoes outside of the low buildings.

Everything had been converted and lived in. Storefronts turned into neighborhood kitchens and toy stores picked clean of usable goods. The tiny apartments that were above the shops had open windows and drying laundry that crisscrossed the street. Sneakers were thrown over cable lines. Candles flickered in the windows.
Ithica looked at him and smiled.

"I've lived in the Standing City," she said, "it's nothing like this." She turned and carried the pot of stew over to a tiny corner home. Looking up at the window, she let out a deep whistle, reminiscent of a wolf call and waited.

Not five seconds later, a pair of heads peeked out from the window.

I. The Pack of Wolves

In all, there were five. But only four lived at home with their mother. Each had the same childlike face as Mathias. Ithica introduced them as the pack of wolves.

They descended on the pot of stew with a scream, a cry, and a shout, rushing upstairs to show their mother the food.

The sound was a shock to Nate's ears. He twitched, looking hard at each one of them and back to Ithica.

"They were with you," he said, "when you found me."

She looked at him with a tilt of her head. "They were the ones who found you, actually. You remember?"

"I remember what they sound like."

"They're loud," She said, with a laugh screaming out at them, "and ungrateful!"

The second to youngest was the only one to stop on the stoop before rushing after his brothers. He looked most like Mathias, with gold-flecked brown hair and bent out-of-shape glasses.

"Thank you, Ithica."

"You're welcome," She shook her head again. "If it wasn't for them, you'd be dead, Nate. Funny how a bunch of kids can change your life that way, right?" There was a slight gleam in her eyes.

Nate said nothing, but he smiled back.

IV. The House of the Silent Skyline

His bedroom was warm at night.

On the mattress, Nate lay out and unfolded the map of the Standing City, staring at it. There didn't seem to be a place like Central Street. Instead, everything was in grids and quarters. Everything perfectly arranged.

All the hope he had seen in the streets earlier, the throngs of people he imagined moving through it had diminished. He only saw cold, calculated lines and the harsh reality of tall buildings and government areas. Nothing drawn in seemed communal. Nothing seemed free.

His heart fell, just a little. He folded the map up and put it away. Closed his eyes and tried to sleep. In a day he felt like he had made friends and lost them, all because of one simple thing.

He tried not to think about it.

* * *

James slipped into the unlocked bedroom in the middle of the night. The sound of the door creaking woke Nate up. He faked he was still asleep, though, with closed eyes and steady breathing. James sat next to him and ignored his facade.

"Nathaniel..." James began.

"Yeah?" Nate groaned.

"Are you going to let me see the map?"

Nate struggled to adjust his eyes to the meager light. Beside him, James crossed his legs.

"I can't," he finally answered.

"Can't or won't?"

"Both."

James let out a sigh. "I've wanted to go back for a while now. Just to see it. Just to see if it has changed much without me there."

"But you have this now," Nate twisted in the bed, sitting halfway up. "I've seen Central Street. And you guys have one another. A family. You're not scared, no one is telling you what you can't do. I think..." Nate frowned, "I think I've wanted the wrong thing for a while now."

"Nate," James said. "You're right, it's wonderful, but...those people, the ones on Central Street? They've never lived in the city. It is a different sort of longing. I love it here, don't get me wrong. I can't stay in the Standing City, but I want to see it again. Ithica doesn't understand, but Mathias does. He didn't say it, but I know he does. That's where he learned everything. That's where I grew up. My family is there. I just want to see it again. Just once."

"You want the map." Nate said, in a tone more knowing than a question.

"I could go with you," James said.

Nate closed his eyes.

"You guys don't stay here all the time, do you? This place seems too sparse for that." When he opened his eyes again, James was nodding. "But you dock often and when you do, you dock here."

"In various parts of the Black City, you're right."

Nate sat up completely. "I'll give you the map if you take me in."

James rose a brow. "The Black City is open to all…"

"I haven't been looking for a city. I've been looking for a family." Nate nodded. He wasn't looking for the sleek lines; he was looking for the warm smiles. James shook his head. He looked away from Nate towards the door.

Nate swallowed, thick and hard in the back of his throat, fearing the worst.

"Out here, you don't have to barter for that. You're already part of our family. The Black City is yours."

Nate remained quiet, looking at his backpack instead of James. A sizzle of electric feeling surged through him. A proper answer, a good answer, and an answer he had been hoping to hear for longer than he cared to count. He was struggling not to jump off the mattress. Instead, he pulled out a key from around his neck and snapped the worn-out leather that bound it to him. Undoing the lock, he pulled out the map.

"In families," Nate whispered, "you share." His eyes connected with James' and James smiled in return. The map shifted hands.

"Nathaniel," James replied, placing the map on his lap, "Welcome home."

Melissa Dominic is a writer, mapmaker and historian of places that don't exist. She was born on the city streets of New Jersey, but now lives in a retirement community just north of Miami, Florida. She has a B.A. in English from Florida International University. Melissa enjoys tea, post-rock, the future, and book art. She is currently working on a full-length serial novel. Her blog can be found at BrokenNerves.Net

Aaron's Unmasking

By
Chuck Robertson

I always enjoyed the moment Mother removed the screws from the mask and took it off my face. The air felt so much more natural than all that bare metal. She ran a damp cloth over my cheeks. The cool water on my skin felt so refreshing, many times better than the inside of the mask that covered it every other time.

I reached my fingers upward, hoping just to get a feel of my real face. Mother applied a gentle touch to move my hand back into its original position.

"Now, now, we don't do that," she said, through her own mask. "Our faces are private, remember?"

Her lips curled up in her mouth slit, and her eyes glistened through their portals. Even when she said no, she always managed to do it with warmth and compassion. Just as I had never seen my naked face, I had never seen hers either, but had every little dent and scratch in the metal of her mask memorized.

"Why, Mother? It's just us. There's nobody else around here who would ever see what we look like."

"It just isn't done, Aaron. Someday you'll understand."

I looked down as far down as I could, but only saw the transparent double-image of my own nose. I couldn't see anything unusual about it. The rest of my face still remained a mystery to me.

Mother patted my cheeks dry with a towel, and all too soon slipped the mask back on and fastened the screws. As a last gesture, she tugged on the straps to make sure they would stay in place.

I walked over to the mirror for a final look before heading off to school. A simple tin mask stared back at me. I had tried my best to make it look better. I loved dogs, and had painted it like the face of one. It was still not my real face, however.

She handed me my lunch.

I looked in the sack. "Potatoes *again*."

"Remember, there are people who don't even have as much as we do."

She sent me to school, kissing the metal covering my cheek. I never felt her lips on my face, of course, but it seemed as if her love seeped from her mouth slit, through my mask, and directly into me. I felt my lips smile, although I had never seen such an expression except in old photos.

I walked down the road, which was hard as a rock but smooth as glass. What I always thought strangest about it, however, was that it had to be ten meters wide. Why anybody would build a road this wide just for horses and people was beyond me.

Trunks of long-dead plants called trees lined the sides of the road. Before the tumors overtook him, Father would tell me stories his father told him, about the trees dominating the countryside. He said they were so numerous they even blocked out the sky, but they couldn't handle the isotopes in the soil and died. I found this hard to believe, but figured it must have been true or my grandfather would never have said it.

The morning chill seeped through my robe as I entered the outskirts of the village. I passed the long-abandoned buildings on the edge of town, which were rotten and falling in. I remembered the time the village constable caught Marcus and I exploring there.

"You know it's dangerous to go into the ruins," he said through the slits in his dark blue mask. "If I catch you here again, I'll tell your parents."

Just the threat of Mother finding out what I had done was enough to stop me from ever doing that again. I never went back.

Large, rusting objects my father had called cars littered the landscape in this part of town. Before he died, he told me more stories, about these cars traveling the wide roads with the speed of the wind. He said they could reach the village from our house in five minutes. I didn't see how they could ever have moved at all, let alone go as fast as he said they did.

I spotted a group of drudges working beside the road ahead, clearing debris into a pile. Mister Johnson stood in the middle of them, keeping a watchful eye as always. He waved at me and I waved back.

One of the drudges broke away from the group and ran at me with his arms spread wide. I felt like running, but noticed Mister Johnson didn't seem too afraid for my safety, so I calmed down.

The drudge hugged me so close that his plain white mask almost touched mine. "I love you," he said with words so slurred I could barely understand them.

"Now, Nelson, how do we greet people?" Mister Johnson said.

The drudge let me go and backed up a step. "How do you do?" He bowed.

I had always admired Mister Johnson. He had so much more patience than anyone else I knew and was really good at working with them. On those days that I didn't want to get up for school, I thought of the drudges. At least I had enough intelligence to go to school, but these poor souls didn't even have that.

I reached the inhabited part of the city and strolled onto the school grounds, early as usual. I started playing with the other children. Marcus spotted me and came over. Even if I had not recognized the hippogriff pattern on his mask, I would have known his limp anywhere.

He grabbed my shoulder and took me aside. "I have something to show you."

He reached into the pocket of his robe and pulled out a screwdriver. I saw from the shape of the head it was not just an ordinary screwdriver. It was one of the special ones used to unfasten the masks about our faces.

I looked around to see if any grown-ups were looking. I was happy to see they were not. "If a teacher finds you with that, you'll get into a whole lot of trouble," I said.

"They'll never know. Meet me during lunch time."

"Why? What are you going to do?"

"You'll see."

Mister Rather, the principal, rang the school bell before I could ask any other questions. I went with Marcus to the sixth grade classroom and we took our seats, across the aisle from each other. Mrs. Grayson started History class before I could prod Marcus for any more information. I hoped he was not intending to actually take off a mask.

I got out my history book and opened it with as much care as I could. The pages were yellow with age, and many of them wanted to fall out on their own. Mrs. Grayson had cautioned us at the beginning of the school year all our books had been printed before the war and were many years old. We had to be careful with them because no one would ever be able to print any more.

The pages of the book were covered with photographs of people, but none of them wore a mask. It also showed pictures of huge cities, packed with pedestrians everywhere. The streets were jammed with cars, so many I couldn't even begin to imagine them moving with the speed of the wind without running into each other. Many days I would think to myself, this is what things looked like before the bombs exploded and left their isotopes everywhere.

Finding Home

We finished our morning classes and the lunch bell rang. I went outside with my sack of potatoes. We had our little group that always sat together. Martha was already there, in her mask with a dragon painted on it. Ann came toward us, her mask now looking like the face of a cat. It seemed she had a different animal every week, but I could always recognize her because her left arm was missing. Seeing her deformity caused me to think of my Mother's words that morning. Yes, all I had to eat that day were potatoes, but at least I had all my limbs. I was sure she would have gladly traded a year of eating potatoes to have her left arm whole.

Marcus limped toward us, reminding me of the screwdriver. I hoped he had forgotten about it, but instead he held it up so everyone could see. "I dare anyone here to let me take their mask off," he said.

Martha said, "Why don't you take yours off!"

We all echoed her suggestion. Marcus was in a corner, but we knew he was too proud to back down. He led us toward the abandoned section of the school building. We stopped when we reached the rope Mister Rather had told us never to cross. Marcus crossed the rope and looked back at us. "Who's the coward now?"

I glanced toward the used part of the building, and saw no one was watching. I crossed, and the girls followed. Marcus spent most of the lunch period fumbling with the screws and finally managed to get one loose. He slipped the mask partway off his face.

Even in the subdued light of the abandoned area, the sight sickened me. Clusters like lumpy modeling clay covered the exposed section of his face, and the skin was a swirl of disfiguration. The girls screamed, and started crying. I felt like throwing my potato lunch back up, and wished with all my heart I had never been there that day.

Mrs. Grayson must have heard the screams, because she ran all the way down the abandoned hall and stood speechless when she saw the cause. She wrapped Marcus in a flap of her robe and whisked him away. She called for Mister Parks, the seventh grade teacher, who herded the rest of us back into the occupied part of the school and to the bench in front of the principal's office.

After what seemed like hours, the door opened and Mister Rather stood over us. "We have something serious to talk about," he said.

We walked in with baby steps. He motioned for us to sit in the chairs in front of his desk as he closed the door. The stern look of his eyes through the slits in his red and silver mask showed this was something more serious than just talking in class. I knew the punishment would have to be severe.

"Has it ever occurred to you that your masks are fastened on for a reason?"

The three of us said "No," at about the same time, even though we all knew full well they would not have made the masks so hard to take off if they didn't intend for them to stay on. "You are all old enough to know you are never allowed to take your masks off, right?"

In unison, we let out a weak "Yes."

"Do you know what a taboo is?"

I answered "No," even though I knew full well the meaning of the word had been discussed many times in all our classes. I somehow hoped playing dumb might get me in a little less trouble.

"A taboo is a rule that must never be broken," he said. "There is a taboo against showing your face to anyone. It is our way of protecting ourselves from each other. What you all did was very bad, don't you agree?"

We let out another collective "Yes."

"As punishment, you are all going to get detention for a month. And one more thing, you are each going to get a note to your parents about this. They need to know about this kind of thing."

I felt almost as bad as I had felt the moment I glimpsed a corner of Marcus's face. I imagined my Mother reading that note. A month's detention would be a play day compared to what she would do to me.

It occurred to me that Marcus was not here. I wondered, if the three of us got a month's worth of detention, what his punishment must have been.

"What will you do with Marcus?" I asked.

"That is between me, him, and his parents. Now go back to your classes, and make sure you drop by my office to pick up your notes before heading home today."

I went through the rest of the day sick with worry about telling Mother about what happened. I wished the day would last forever, so that I wouldn't have to face her at the end of it, but school let out anyway.

I took a lot of time getting home after school, trying to put off showing Mother that note as long as possible. I was careful to be quiet when I walked into our house, and didn't announce myself like I usually did.

Mother's bedroom door was open when I got there. She had her back to me, but was looking into the mirror with her mask off. I just stood and stared for a moment. I had to know, did she look like Marcus too, underneath that mask? Did I look like him? Did everybody look like him?

I crept upon her, hoping for just a glance at her face. A board under my feet creaked at the last minute. She jumped and slapped her mask back over her face before I even got a look at it. She turned around. Although all I could see was the whites of her eyes, I could tell there was more anger there than I could remember in a long time. "Don't ever walk in on me like that again!"

Since she was already angry, I thought it was a good time to show her the note. I handed it to her without a word. I watched her eyes travel from one end of the paper to the other as she read every line carefully. When she was done, she let out an "Oh My, Oh My. Aaron, I am so disappointed. You are going to have to stop hanging around that Marcus boy, he's such a bad influence on you."

That evening, neither one of us talked while we ate our supper. I wasn't very hungry after thinking about Marcus's face, or the shame of being in so much trouble. I could only guess at the thoughts that must be going through Mother's head.

My hands were also shaking so hard, I couldn't help but get as much soup on my mask as I was able to shovel through my narrow mouth slit. I stared at Mother's mask, and then put a hand to mine. I agonized to know what was behind all that metal.

"Mother, do grown-ups ever take their masks off and look at their own faces?" I asked.

"Of course they do, but it is always in private. They never let anyone else see their faces."

"Will I ever be allowed to see my face?"

"Yes, Aaron, when you are old enough to understand that you are not to show yours to anyone."

"So no one has ever seen your face? Not even Father, when he was alive?"

"Your father and I saw each other's faces from time to time. But that is different. A husband and wife have a very special relationship. We never showed our faces to anyone else, though."

I felt my pulse throb faster. My face perked up inside the metal covering it.

"What did Father's face look like? What does your face look like? What does mine look like? Do we all look like Marcus?"

"Aaron, hasn't this thing about the masks caused you enough trouble already? Tomorrow, I'm going to have to think up a lot of extra chores for you as punishment for what happened today. I hope you don't think any more about this until you are much, much older."

Before bedtime, Mother got ready to wash my face again. She assembled the water bowl and a screwdriver. My heart beat faster with each screw that fell. When the last one was removed, she pulled the mask off. Instinct drove me to put a hand toward my face, but Mother gently pushed it down. Then I did something I had never done before, I tried a second time to touch my face. She grabbed my wrist with a firmer grip this time.

"Aaron, you know that's a naughty area," she said.

Finding Home

Her words, gentle and loving as they were, were no longer enough to restrain me.

"Mother, I can't go on not knowing what I look like. If you don't let me see my face today, I swear I'll take it off myself sometime when you aren't around."

Mother paused for a minute. Her eyes seemed to fog up from inside her eye portals, like she was in deep thought. "I knew this moment would happen someday. You need to understand, Aaron, once you look at your face, there's no going back. You can't un-remember something."

"I'm going to find out someday."

"Yes, you are, Aaron, but you have so much growing to do yet. The masks are an issue even for us adults."

"Haven't you told me I'm growing up faster than you ever thought? I might as well see my face sooner than later."

She took a deep breath in, and slowly let it out. "Very well, walk over to the mirror and see for yourself."

Fear, doubt, and anticipation entered my head, all at the same time. Anxiety settled into my stomach until it felt like a sack of grain. I smelled a sweaty odor surrounding me.

With the straps unfastened, it would only take me a second to pull my mask off. For one moment I thought about giving up the idea and letting Mother re-fasten the screws. Then, I suppressed the doubts and slid it away.

The face in the mirror that stared back at me was not what I expected at all. There were no clumps of matter or spiraling ridges. My face was perfect, just like all the ones in the history books. There were no deformities whatsoever.

I ran my hands over my bare face for the first time in my life. The skin felt something like rubber, but warm. I gathered a pinch of the skin between my thumb and forefinger. It hurt a little bit.

Glee overwhelmed me as soon I realized I was unaffected by the radiation. I laughed out loud and jumped around. I felt so relieved to know I had a perfect face after all!

I looked over and noticed Mother was not sharing my joy. Instead, she unfastened the straps on her mask and let it fall. All the excitement from the previous moment left me when I saw her naked face. It was deformed like Marcus'. I felt sick inside, partly at her appearance, and partly because I didn't consider all the other people who were not as lucky as me.

"Oh, Mother, I'm sorry I acted so happy, I never considered all the others who are different from me. I feel bad now, I should have thought."

"Don't feel that way, Aaron, I'm happy for you. Seeing you grow up to be a healthy young man has been the highlight of my life. It was me who wanted to show you my face."

"Why?"

"To let you know that the radiation affects everyone differently. It doesn't know any boundaries. It would divide friends, families, everyone."

"Even my friends and I?"

"It doesn't have to, Aaron. With the masks, we are unaware of our differences. That's why we wear them."

I thought of mother, going through life knowing about the differences between us but never letting on. I also thought about Marcus and Ann. I always knew about their physical deformities, but they hardly ever came to mind because of their robes. It never occurred to me before today that their faces could be so different from mine as well. I wondered, did Martha and Ann have normal faces, or were they deformed like Marcus and Mother? I realized more clearly than ever that I didn't even want to know.

Mother set her mask back over her face and fastened the straps.

I had to admit I was happier to see her that way because I was not reminded of our differences. As much as I hated my mask, I slipped it back onto my face. I tried to fasten it, but couldn't see the screws behind my head.

Mother noticed my difficulty. She moved to get a clearer view. "Here, Aaron, let me help you get the mask back on."

Finding Home

Chuck Robertson is the son of a geologist and a registered nurse. As a teenager, he spent many hours reading Clarke, Asimov, and Heinlein and wanted to become the next Isaac Asimov. He soon discovered there is a lot more to writing than just putting words on paper. He tried writing off and on several times throughout his life but other things kept getting in the way. After many years, he has finally acquired the discipline and maturity necessary to become a serious writer and is currently pursuing that goal.

    He graduated from Missouri State University. He started his career as a science teacher but is now employed in the information systems field.

    He has been married for seventeen years to a registered nurse and compassionate wife and mother. Together, they are raising two brilliant and (mostly) well-behaved teenage children. When not working, doing family things or writing he likes to build military models or play with model trains.

    He feels privileged to have been born and raised in the Missouri Ozarks. He continues to live there, which he and his wife find a very beautiful place to be. More than all this, he has been blessed with a wonderful family and is living a happy life with them.

Affirmations

By
S.R. Algernon

"I have absolutely no intention of robbing Burger Bastion," said Thomas Rensch. He faced the scanner, which was a squat machine next to the booth's inner set of doors. It looked like an ATM, except for the eye—a fish-eye camera lens flanked by LEDs—just above the touchscreen display. The Burger Bastion logo, a gargantuan cheeseburger encircled by a cartoon stone wall, floated like a screensaver on the display while the computer pondered Thomas's statement.

"Response not accepted," said the booth. The computer twittered, and the light flashed red.

Thomas sighed and looked back at the line behind him, on the other side of the booth's acrylic glass outer doors. Three men in business suits and a suntanned woman stood on the sidewalk. One of the men accidentally made eye contact before hurriedly glancing up at the overcast sky, as if he were inspecting the city's geodesic dome for cracks.

Thomas took a deep breath, looked straight at the camera and tried again.

"I do not intend to rob this restaurant or do anything else illegal while on the premises," he said, straining to keep his voice level and subdued.

"Response not accepted."

Thomas sucked in a breath through his teeth and let it out slowly. That was his third attempt. After a fourth failure, the booth would lock him inside. He would have to wait until a security officer showed up and cleared him to leave. Thomas pushed the cancel button, not wanting to jeopardize his orange-level clearance.

He weighed the options of having food delivered and walking to a vending machine until he heard someone knocking on the booth. He turned to see young woman standing on the other side of the doors and pointing to the door handle.

Thomas flushed with embarrassment. People usually ignored each other they were waiting for the booth, especially when someone was "talking to the eye." Still, Thomas could not blame her for wanting to cut ahead. At least she had the courtesy not to speak, lest the booth treat her words as Thomas's fourth affirmation.

"Sorry," said Thomas, as he opened the booth's outer door.

"Don't worry." She examined the booth for a moment, took a few sheets of paper out of her pocket and flipped through them. Each was a little bit larger than a fortune cookie slip. She handed one to Thomas. "Here. Try this. I'm Sophie, by the way."

Thomas nodded and examined the paper. One side read SOPHIE JACOBS, JERICHO COMMUNITY PROJECT. The other side had a short sentence. Thomas reentered the booth and read the sentence aloud.

"I hereby affirm that I will abide by federal, state and municipal regulations while on these premises."

"Affirmation accepted."

Sophie made it through the booth on her first try and followed Thomas inside.

"What...was that?" said Thomas. He thought of saying 'Thank you' but stopped himself. If she had tricked the booth somehow, and if security thought that he had put her up to it, they might wind up charging him as an accomplice.

"The affirmation booths," said Sophie, "are trained with sample sentences before they go on the market. If your affirmation is similar enough to one of the training sentences, the computer is a little more tolerant. Besides, reading someone else's words is a good way to keep your voice even. The booths take a dim view of prosody."

"But, how?"

"If you really want to know, my mother helped design the voice recognition algorithms for the booths. But that's not what I wanted to talk to you about. I'll wait at the table by the corner while you order."

"Aren't you...?" Thomas gestured at the menu. He felt a little strange asking the question, or talking to anyone at dinnertime, for that matter. Most evenings, he took a seat by the window and watched the train go by as he ate.

"Not yet. I have a few more meetings this evening."

Thomas sat down in the booth with a burger and a small drink. He did not feel much like eating either. *What was she up to?*

"Do you feel safe here?" she asked.

"What do you mean?"

"I mean, do you feel safer talking to me now that we've gone through that booth?"

"I guess so. Well, not really." Thomas chewed thoughtfully. "You ask a lot of questions about, you know, talking to the eye."

"I just want to find out more about your experience. You feel safe in here. That booth keeps the looters and vandals and terrorists out, right? That booth keeps this place from turning into the terrible city that your parents told you stories about. When the booth flashes red, does that make you feel cut off from that safety?"

"Are you...selling something?" said Thomas. The ones selling vacation packages always asked about how nervous you were. He turned his attention to the burger, away from the onslaught of conversation.

Finding Home

"Not exactly. To be honest, I'm buying something. Or maybe asking a favor. You work at YOURnet, right? Are your subscribers nervous, too? Are they more nervous than they were five or ten years ago?"

"Our customer data is confidential," said Thomas automatically. So that was it, thought Thomas. *A rival company lining up customers. How did she ever get past the booth?* "I'm sorry, but I should go."

"Wait," said Sophie. "We just want to help."

"Are you from Counseling Services or something? Look, I don't have a problem, OK, and neither does anyone at YOURnet. I just had a little trouble getting in the front door. It isn't any of your business." A few of the other customers turned to stare, and Thomas lowered his voice. "I've got to go."

Thomas went down to the city park to jog for a half hour before he felt ready to face the booth at his apartment. The green light came as such a relief that he stayed in all weekend to avoid giving the booth a chance to change its mind. He used his orange clearance to access the video archives and watched the old performances. Robert De Niro, Jim Carrey and Lucille Ball filled his wall screen, with the sound piped in through headphones so that the neighbors wouldn't suspect.

The beaming faces, grimaces and gesticulations were as alien to Thomas as a lion's toothy yawn, but it fascinated him to think that humans were capable of such things, even though he knew they were only acting. The video archive chased away thoughts of affirmations and performance quotas until Monday morning, when the cycle started again.

* * *

"Affirmation not accepted. Please repeat."

"I will not commit any illegal activity while inside the YOURnet building."

"Affirmation not accepted. Please repeat."

Thomas took a half-step backward and took a deep breath. He hunched his shoulders, staring at the tile floor through the glass door. He thought about the weather—dry, cold and overcast—and spoke the affirmation that Sophie had given him.

"Statement accepted."

Thomas walked to his cubicle in silence, just like every other day. Thomas did not mind his job. It kept him busy and no one bothered him, except for the weekly motivational e-mails from his boss. YOURnet sifted through the wilds of the internet, ferried appropriate content through the city's firewall, and delivered it to each subscriber according to his or her profile. Thomas was there to catch the computer's mistakes, like the time when it decided that "white power" was some sort of alternative energy. Red flag. Green flag. Click, click, click for eight hours.

Usually, it required no thought at all, but after his conversation with Sophie, he noticed something strange. He turned to Frank in the next cubicle over.

"Hey, Frank. Have you ever noticed, people's profiles, they don't change? They do the same thing, week after week, always alone?"

"So?" said Frank, without looking up from his terminal.

"Doesn't it strike you as strange?"

"If it's the sorting algorithm, talk to the software people. We just approve content."

Thomas went back to work. News stories, video clips and ads scrolled by. Click. Click. Today, Thomas added a few items of his own under ACTIVITIES, along with the usual online games, solitary hobbies and—for the adventurous—excursions to an uncontaminated beach or hiking trail. Thomas added tips, like, "Find out if any of your neighbors likes opera too," or "Why not go to the concert this time instead of streaming the video?" He hoped to prove Sophie wrong. *We don't have a problem with the booths*, he thought. *They're a tool, not something we hide behind.* Thomas abandoned his impromptu experiment when he fell behind on his quota, and by lunchtime he had forgotten about it.

A few times that afternoon, Thomas caught Frank glancing furtively in his direction between bouts of typing. Later, an e-mail arrived from Counseling Services telling him to report in by the end of the day to discuss his "at risk" behavior. He noticed that three of the banner ads on his e-mail had quietly switched to anti-anxiety drugs during the afternoon. Thomas deleted the Counseling Services e-mail and sweated out the last fifteen minutes of his shift. His relief at making it out the door without a demerit or a trip to a padded cell lasted only as long as his walk to the train platform.

A news alert interrupted the usual rotation of overhead video ads on the overhead screens.

"Counseling Services are treating two men," said a tranquil synthetic voice, "following an outbreak of aggression within the Harmony Grove apartment complex. Residents reported that the two men engaged in a loud and protracted altercation over which of two soccer teams was superior to the other. The complex manager reassured distressed residents that the apartment booths are being updated to prevent another incident. YOURnet representatives offered no comment on the rumor that policy violations by a YOURnet employee contributed to the incident."

Thomas huddled in the booth, cringing at the thought that his face could appear on the train's overhead TV screens at any time. He imagined the announcer's soothing voice: "Authorities have identified Thomas Rensch, an employee of YOURnet, as the source of the unapproved content. If you see him, please contact your nearest security officer or press the ALERT button in any affirmation booth."

Thomas stepped into the booth that led to the turnstiles. The train platform was only level blue, so the booths there hardly ever gave anyone any trouble.

"I affirm that I will not do anything illegal while I'm on the train."

"Affirmation not accepted."

"I hereby affirm that I will abide by federal, state and municipal regulations while on these premises."

"Affirmation not accepted."

"What do you mean? I take this train every day. Let me in."

"Affirmation not accepted."

Last chance, thought Thomas. Thomas pushed the button and waited until his card came back out.

"To hell with you," he said, as he stormed out of the booth. Would Robert DeNiro or James Dean have put up with this?

"Wait!" said the affirmation booth. Its red eye flashed in double time. "Your voice patterns indicate a dangerous level of hostility and anxiety. Remain where you are until a Counseling Services van arrives."

Now what? Thomas stared at the booth in disbelief.

"Attention, rail passengers," the tranquil voice called out over the loudspeaker. "Please be aware that loitering is not permitted in the station perimeter. Passengers must exit the station or ascend to the train platform in five minutes."

Thomas had heard that announcement several times a day, but he had never thought it applied to him. He ran to a nearby directory assistance console, covering his face as he approached, just in case its camera software decided to rat him out to Security.

"Computer," he said. "Search for Jericho Community Project."

"Listing found. Distance: 8.9 kilometers. Please see the map below."

"Copy, please," said Thomas. *Almost nine kilometers. Is the city really that big?*

"Please insert your Citizen ID card for download." The directory assistance computer would certainly be onto him once it read his card. Thomas was about to run when he remembered a voice command from an old movie.
"Printed copy, please," said Thomas. Thomas grabbed the printout and ran. Fortunately, most of the route ran parallel to the rail line, where nobody would notice one more pedestrian in the crowd. After a few kilometers, he veered onto an access road that led to a support beam for the dome. Thomas kept his head down, hoping that nobody would notice a panting man in a sweaty dress shirt. Luckily, the path led into a wide tunnel, where the dim light gave him a little cover. *Only 3.2 kilometers to go.*

Thomas's optimism faded when the tunnel narrowed and he found himself face to face with a row of police officers, each in body armor and riot gear. Each officer stood next to a metal turnstile.

"Identification card," said the one officer.

Thomas considered running. His legs stumbled backward two steps as if to give him a head start, but eventually he handed over his card. He hoped they would simply hold him until Counseling Services arrived instead of charging him for fleeing the booth.

The guard nodded and waved him through.

"No booth?" said Thomas. The officer seemed suddenly puzzled and wary, and Thomas broke into a cold sweat.

"Never mind," said Thomas as he hurried through the turnstile, not turning around until he heard footsteps behind him.

"Hey, man! What did you do that for?"

Thomas turned toward the voice and saw a man in a red jumpsuit.

"Huh?"

"You want them to start giving us a hard time or something? Everyone knows they don't give a damn about you when you're leaving."

"Right. Sorry," said Thomas. He resumed his earlier jogging pace and kept his eyes on the expanding glow in the distance.

At the end of the tunnel, the light was bright enough that he averted his eyes for a moment. Looking back on it from the outside, the cavernous tunnel now seemed like a pore on a vast plane of steel. Thomas had never seen it before, but he knew in an instant that he had just passed through the City Wall.

No. It can't be...

Thomas put his hands up over his nose and mouth as he turned toward the dusty overcast sky. Shouts, clanging, the roar of engines and a thousand other sounds struck Thomas's ears like a wave. Up ahead, an overpass ended in a pile of rubble that someone had fashioned into a crude ramp. Rusty ladders hung from the guardrails down to ground level. A tangle of green covered most of the buildings and had taken over parts of the asphalt.

That's absurd, thought Thomas, *Why on Earth would these Jericho people put their office…outside…?*

"I'll never get there through all this," muttered Thomas as he looked for a street sign that had not been carted off as scrap metal.

"Hey!" A man who'd been squatting near the tunnel entrance called out as he jumped to his feet. "The name's Dominic. I'll get you where you need to go." He led Thomas over to what looked like a trash heap spread out over a blue tarp.

"GPS?" said Thomas.

"Even better," said Dominic, as he pointed out a folded-up sheet of paper. "You don't have to worry about batteries or lost signals with this. Just twenty five Frankies and it's yours."

"Twenty five what?"

"Frankies. Twenty five hundred dollars."

"I don't know what those are. I've got a cash chip."

"New City creds? Sorry, man, but my reader's broke today. How about a trade for that watch you're wearing? I'll even throw in a filter mask for no charge 'cause the strap's broken."

"Fine." Thomas handed over his watch and hurried off, holding the map in one hand and pressing the mask to his face with the other.

Once he found Sophie, he told himself, things would be all right.

* * *

The address on the printout was in a row of small buildings behind an overgrown parking lot. Hand-painted signs read, GUEST WORKER PASSES HERE, TRAINING CENTER and STU'S KITCHEN. One of the storefronts had a gas can and a bicycle wheel hung up where the sign would go. As Thomas approached the JERICHO COMMUNITY PROJECT, he saw the bars over the window and doors and a sign: OPEN FROM 8AM TO 5PM MON WED FRI.

Finding Home

Thomas sat down on a concrete barrier in the parking lot. *A night in jail or a padded room would be better than this. Maybe I really am crazy.* He was about to walk back to the wall and turn himself in to the guards when a bearded man with bare tattooed arms shuffled up to him.

"Do you have any money for the bus?" His voice had a booming, singsong quality—like Dominic's, but while Dominic reminded Thomas of a carnival barker, this man sounded like a pro wrestling announcer. He could not shake the feeling that he had wandered into a movie set.

This was how it went down in the movies, thought Thomas. *First they ask for change or cigarettes. Then the knives came out.*

"Not a single Frankie," he said, bracing himself.

"Me neither. If you're going to hole up here for the night, you'd better get out of sight before the sun gets too far down. And see if you can dig up some better shoes. Those things look like they won't last the week."

"Thanks," said Thomas. He circled behind the strip mall, looking out for attackers. He found a little glass-and-steel booth near a few rusted out gas pumps and figured it might be a directory kiosk. Thomas braced himself against an odor halfway between compost and urine before stepping inside.

"I affirm that I will abide by all rules of the…um… Global Telephone and Telegraph Corporation."

The phone booth did not reply. He tried typing his identification number on the metal keypad, but that did not work either. Finally, he noticed what looked like a microphone or speaker apparatus hanging from a silver cord. *Aha!*

"Directory assistance please. Sophie Jacobs."

The phone said nothing.

"I think this thing is broken."

Thomas let the phone receiver drop. As he did so, he noticed a battered book on the shelf underneath the phone. It read 2023 TELEPHONE DIRECTORY. He flipped to "J" and found S JACOBS at 14 Pioneer Lane. Deciding that it was better to risk walking past nightfall than to spend the night in the parking lot, Thomas circled Pioneer Lane on his map and resumed his walk.

* * *

House number 14 stood out among the three other remaining houses on Pioneer Lane. Instead of an overgrown lawn, Thomas saw a small orchard and a sprawling vegetable garden. Covered walkways topped with solar panels meandered out from the house between the rows of vegetation. A sheet of glass bounded each side of each walkway, sealing it against wind and dirt. The house itself glowed softly through several bay windows and a dozen irregularly-placed, domed skylights.

All that glass and not a single broken window, thought Thomas, as he climbed the steps to the front porch. He saw a soft, steady yellow light coming from a plastic oval next to the door. He faced it and readied an affirmation.

"I, Thomas Rensch, affirm that I will not do anything dangerous or illegal while on these premises."

The yellow oval did nothing. Thomas tapped it with his finger to wake it up, and it emitted a cheerful ding-dong. *Amazing,* thought Thomas. *Even the affirmations are musical here.*

"I'm coming, I'm coming," called a voice, even more musical than the doorbell. The voice was not Sophie's.

"I'm just here to see Sophie," said Thomas, speaking through the door as the he heard the sound of locks being turned and chains rattling.

The plump woman who opened the door took a moment to size him up before opening the door all the way.

"Sophie hasn't lived here in years. I'm Sarah Jacobs, her mother. Come on inside."

"Are you sure? There's no booth out here."

"Doesn't matter," said Mrs. Jacobs, tapping her forehead. "I've got a pretty good one right up here. Come on in and have a seat."

Thomas stepped into a tidy living room. The seamless fusion of old and new struck him at a glance. The wooden table, the chairs and the sofa had the functional, solid look that dated them to well before the wars; but the membrane TV on the far wall displayed an assortment of modern channels, widgets and apps. The room radiated a warm glow that was more than just the skylight. Patches of light and dark floated across the ceiling like passing clouds.

"It's fiber optics," said Mrs. Jacobs. "Bill made it. It catches light from all over the roof and sends it where it's needed."

"But...isn't it dangerous having all this equipment out here?"

"I knew that would be the first thing on your mind. You're from the new city, aren't you? I can tell from your voice. Flat. Expressionless. Once, I might have said robotic, but I've built robots that emote more. Not that I blame you. We do what we have to. But it doesn't have to be that way. You're free now."

"I don't know what you mean."

"Listen to yourself, dear. You haven't been out of the new city more than a few days, and already you're having a conversation, with full sentences and the normal social niceties. Maybe even a little inflection. You've been itching to do more than string words together. You want to express yourself." Mrs. Jacobs smiled.

"I'd settle for a way to get back home and get on with my life. My shift starts at eight tomorrow and I've got a problem, you know, getting through the front door."

"The booths are the real problem. When we first designed them, the old cities were in chaos. Desperate, deranged survivors from the war threatened to overwhelm us. We thought that if we insulated the new cities and gave people the sense that they were safe in their homes and communities, that they would keep that sense of trust. Later on, as we rebuilt our civilization, they would remind us how to trust one another again."

"And we are safe," said Thomas. "I haven't had a problem in years. If I can just get this anxiety under control, I'd be fine. Maybe the counseling appointment was the right idea after all."

Mrs. Jacobs stopped smiling. "Let me finish. Please. We programmed the detectors to match the meaning of the affirmation to the acoustic cues—tone of voice, prosody, signs of stress and so on—in order to distinguish normal from pathological or deceptive speech. Since we knew that speech patterns would change over time, we programmed them to adapt over the years.

"We assumed that a calm, sane human being would produce speech that we considered normal. We didn't realize how the machines would shape you. Within a decade, people in new cities all over the world had stripped their speech of nuance, inflection, or anything that might trigger a red light from the machines. Eventually, this caricature of speech became the mark of a sane, civilized person, and people forgot what speech used to be. As speech became less meaningful, people simply stopped talking. You're probably too young to remember." She paused.

"I've seen it in movies," Thomas volunteered.

"The movies! Yes! That explains your progress. With a little help, you could break free of the conditioning altogether. That's why we started Jericho in the first place, to bring down the walls." Mrs. Jacobs paused. "I know this is a personal question, but is your family back in the new city?"

"My parents died in the last war. There really isn't anyone else."

"Then why not stay here? I used to take on boarders when the refugees came through. There's plenty of room in the guesthouse. Jericho would pay for food and anything else you needed. All we ask is that you let me record your speech as you develop a normal speech repertoire. What we learn from you could help us treat others. You could be the key to keeping our species whole."

"You're asking me to give up my job, my apartment, everything. I can't. I don't know why yet, but I just can't."

"It's late. All I can ask you to do is sleep on it. I'll show you to the guesthouse. There's a lead-lined tunnel connecting it to the main house. Bill was always worried about the radiation. He tried so hard to keep the dust out."

"Bill?" said Thomas. "Is that Sophie's father? He's a genius."

"He'd have been glad to hear that," said Mrs. Jacobs, "particularly from you."

"Me?"

"Bill always hoped that someone would remember him for more than the walls and the checkpoints. He wanted to save the world once, just like I did. The new city was supposed to be our sanctuary. Then, bit-by-bit, he saw it turning into a prison, and it never gave him a moment's peace after that. That's why we need you, Thomas. We need to know that the damage we'd done might still be undone."

"I'm sorry," said Thomas. He had promised to sleep on the decision, but he knew that he had made up his mind—even if he did not quite know why.

* * *

Thomas awoke the next morning with dreams of a giant spider—the mutants from the old movies—fresh in his mind. He had been running through the rubble along with a screaming throng, and his only thought had been finding someplace safe. In the guesthouse, the light of dawn through the window cast a lattice pattern on the wall, almost like a web. The more Thomas thought about it, the more the house reminded him of a giant spider, with the covered walkways for legs and the assortment of skylight eyes. Thomas wondered if the dream meant that Jericho had caught him in its web for the sake of Mrs. Jacobs's research, but something else in this building provoked his desire to leave.

Before Thomas had a chance to puzzle out the dream, a bicycle pulled up outside. He rolled out of bed, changed back into his clothes and walked around the side of the house to see who it was. Sophie stood on the front porch wearing goggles and a filter mask. She wore a backpack and carried two other packages in her hands.

"Thomas!" said Sophie, "They said you were here, but I didn't quite believe it."

"I didn't plan on it. The booths kept me from..."

The front door opened.

"Good morning," said Mrs. Jacobs. "I can see that you've already met."

"So, did my mother give you the spiel? Are you going to help her out with the research?"

"I thought about it," said Thomas, "but I can't stay. I just don't fit in here. I can't talk the way you do. I'm just not cut out to be Eliza Doolittle right now."

"I wish you would reconsider," said Sophie. "The world isn't as bad as it used to be. There's more out here than you think. Look around you. Is it really such a scary place?"

"It's not that," said Thomas. "I think being here made me realize why I have to go back. I know about your father. I know that he wanted to be remembered for what he built. Well, he will be. He created a human world behind those walls, not a world at the mercy of disease and radiation. If we're going to survive, we have to remember that we can still build, not merely survive. The booths aren't just about keeping us safe. They remind us that the new city—just like this house—is worth protecting."

"Then you'll go back to the new city…to help us rebuild the old one?" asked Sophie.

"I just realized that the city doesn't have to be a cocoon. It can be a web too, pulling in people from all over the world and bringing their ideas together."

"I've tried," said Sophie, "but it's been so hard to convince people that it's safe to let us back in."

"We don't need to feel safer. We just need to remember how life used to be, and that it was worth the risk. After that, no walls will be able to stop us. Or you. But that can't happen unless I get back through the gate."

"I think I can help." Sophie took a box of blank white cards out of her backpack and handed one to Thomas. "Hold this about a meter from your face and keep it steady." It flashed, and his picture appeared in the upper right corner.

"That's a guest worker card. It will only get you blue-level clearance. It won't get you into your old apartment or your office, but it will get you through the gate."

"Thanks," said Thomas, "to both of you. And as for conversation, you can have all you want. Call me anytime."

"And we'll be waiting," said Sophie, "in case you get the urge to explore."

* * *

The immigration process—physical exam, decontamination, psych profiling and background check—felt remote, as if Thomas were just auditioning for a role. Thomas endured the scanners and the interrogation machines until they let him back into the tunnel, a free man.

He used the guest pass to board the train, but he knew that the real challenge was the YOURnet office. He felt the old jitters return as he took out his real identification card. RENSCH, THOMAS, it read. Thomas could not help thinking that the man looking back at him was a stranger, or at least an old friend that he had lost touch with over the years.

Outside his office, a crowd filled the street. Bewildered riot police circled the crowd in an effort to contain it. *Were they protesting YOURnet?* Tom wondered. He hurried around them, trying to hide his face as he ducked into the nearest booth.

"I affirm that I will not violate any YOURnet policies while I am here." His voice felt lighter and young, if a little hoarse from overuse.

"Affirmation not accepted. Please repeat."

"I hereby affirm that I will abide by federal, state and municipal regulations while on these premises."

"Affirmation not accepted. Please repeat."

Drat, thought Thomas, even the old template didn't work. Thomas remembered what Mrs. Jacobs had said. The booth learned from its experiences. Old affirmations that nobody used anymore might still be pristine in its memory banks.

"I, Thomas Rensch, swear to uphold the ideals of safety, truth and justice. I will not waver in my dedication to our valued customers. So help me God."

Thomas remembered things like that from the movies, but he reminded himself that the movies weren't real. He cleared his throat.

"I affirm that I will do my best to make my customers' lives a little brighter and try not to get on my co-workers' nerves too much. I'll follow the rules, and if I make a mistake I'll own up to it. That's really the best I can do." The words slipped out before he had a chance to force them into their approved shape and rhythm. His voice sounded slovenly and unhinged. Thomas's shoulders slumped. If they had not revoked his orange clearance by now, this recording might seal the deal.

The booth mulled it over.

"Affirmation accepted."

"Thank you," said Thomas, "and have a nice day."

* * *

At the office, Thomas's co-workers pressed their faces against the window, watching the crowd in silence. Thomas joined them. From here, he could see over the heads of the spectators to an open space about thirty meters long. Two men in t-shirts were trying to dribble a soccer ball past one another and kick it through the goalposts they had made by dragging garbage cans into position. The only sound was from the scuffing of their running shoes against the pavement and the occasional hollow boomph of the ball when one of them ventured a kick.

"Thomas?"

Thomas turned and saw his boss standing in amazement in his office doorway.

"You're…late. Work?" he said. He seemed to regret the vocal outburst and backed into his office to write an e-mail like a normal person.

"Had a little trouble with the booth."

"There's no need to…um… Here. Read this."

Thomas's boss opened an e-mail onto the wall screen in his office and beckoned him into his office to read it.

MEMO TO SUPERVISORY STAFF
In the past 24 hours, 514 positive subscriber comments were received following incidents of non-virtual interaction in the YOURnet service area. We are investigating the feasibility of implementing non-virtual content as part of the YOURnet package. Support staff should be aware of this development and assemble relevant customer data before the next leadership meeting.

"Can you help with this?"

"I can suggest some activities that some of our customers might like to do together. They could start by watching the soccer match outside."

"Yes. Very good work, Thomas. Very, um..." The boss hesitated, and then carefully raised his hand in a slow-motion underhand karate chop.

Thomas picked up on the gesture, reached out, and shook his hand. "Thank you, sir," said Thomas. "I'll do my best. You can count on it."

Outside, a cheer sputtered to life through the crowd. It was not quite like vintage soccer announcers, but there was a hint of old-time melody to it—even if the sound was closer to Bob Dylan than James Brown or Ethel Merman.

GOOOOAAALLLL!

We might not have reached the goal yet, thought Thomas, *but at least now I've got a good look at the goalposts.*

S. R. Algernon

S. R. Algernon has been interested in science fiction since childhood, growing up on Asimov, Bradbury, OrwelII and other writers a generation or two before his. He has written fiction since the late 1990s, when he studied creative writing at the University of North Carolina at Chapel Hill. Since then, he has studied 20th century Japanese science fiction and lived in Japan on two occasions. Currently, I reside in Singapore, with the aim of incorporating social and technological changes in Southeast Asia into my writing.

"Affirmations" is his first paid sale, although he is optimistic about several pieces of flash fiction and short stories currently under consideration. He has been a member of the critters.org writing workshop for the past few years. Current writing projects include several short stories and a few novels in progress. His reading and writing interests include hard science fiction, historical fiction, Asian science fiction and works that address social and political themes, with the occasional dabbling in horror and satirical fiction.

Story

By
Butch Kenney

"Sto-ry…Sto-ry…Sto-ry…"

It's like this every Seventh Night.

"Story…Story…" The chant starts off slow and soft.

Then it gets louder and they start to clap their hands and stomp their feet. Soon the entire amphitheater is on its feet, shouting and cheering. The structure, built against a man-made berm of dirt and debris, would look quite familiar to any ancient Roman. Only, in place of stone benches, grassy terraces had been formed and tended to by different holdfasts from the commune. Some swaths of green grass were decorated with benches cobbled together from the concrete and steel leavings from a previous civilization. Others tended with care with to small flowers that make up a loose boundary between holdfasts.

The old man cracks a smile. He had been feigning sleep and now he acts startled, yawns theatrically and slowly stands up, stretching out old muscles gone tight from sitting for too long. He's done this for years. The only thing that changes is time. Different children in the seats, but they are still the youngest of the commune. He grows older; the children's faces change.

Hunched over and moving slowly, he walks through the crowd. Stopping here and there to pat one child on the head, pausing to cup another's face in his old hands. He has smiles for all of them. He knows them all. If anyone was the wiser, they would see the pattern he makes walking through them. No one knows though. He is Story, and he alone holds that knowledge.

Slowly, he makes his way from his honored seat among the young children of the crèche, down and around to the back of the large semicircular stage. His chair is brought out and a few logs are added to the fire bowl in front of him. His shadow is thrown against the stage curtain, growing larger as he approaches the chair placed just in front of the flames. He lowers his old frame into the chair, moving a few cushions around to help support his back.

When he first sat in this chair, it seemed too small to hold him. Now, he is dwarfed by the high back and wide seat. If not for the cushions of goose feathers to prop him up, he would look like a child, not a revered elder of one of the larger communes of the central coastal area. On cue, the crowd sits down and a hush falls. Soon, it's as quiet as a tomb. One deep breath, then another.

He starts to feel around his threadbare robes, nervously searching for something. "Well, it seems I have as many holes as pockets."

The children in front giggle.

Then someone shouts out, "The day the steel fell, tell us of that day." Then another shouts, "The countries, again, tell of the falls." Still another shouts out, "The end, the end—tell of that, Story." Then it's a jumble of loud voices: "The steel, the falls, the end," over and over.

Then he raises his hand.

Slowly the crowd falls silent again.

"My name is Story." That's how he starts every Seventh Night. It's not as much a name as it is a job, a lifelong task to teach and keep his children safe. Tonight, what he says to the people of the town will be something few, if any, have heard before. None since he took up the mantel of Story would have heard, that he knows for sure.

* * *

"Long before The Fall…" the old man begins his Telling. He starts with the familiar lessons that many of the young and all of the old have heard so many times it has become a second nature to them. Ideals like "stewardship," "honor" and "trust" become a pattern for the children much like a lattice trains a rosebush.

Then, abruptly, he switches focus to the values and ideals of those that lived before The Fall. "Greed drove all people in that dark time. They created families that enforced an unnatural pairing—for life—of a man and a woman, a husband and a wife. More often than not, greed would drive one of them to destroy that which they had created. This would often disrupt the entire cycle of nurturing we use in the crèches, dooming the children to a tortured life."

He pauses here, trying to catch his breath, his conflicting emotions written on his face, perhaps hidden in the dancing light of the fire bowls at his feet.

That wasn't always the case though. Many families didn't end in catastrophe and had wonderful children raised in a nurturing environment. But that's not the story I'm here to tell.

"Greed drove families together. Family groups became towns and villages. Then, always wanting more, these towns and villages became cities of steel and concrete, each one needing to be more magnificent than the last. Nations were built up around these monstrous cities. Nations desired what others had and what they lacked. Armies were raised to protect the treasure and resources either raped from the land or plundered in brutal conquest."

Of course, another simplification, but something easily remembered and thus learned. Though, nothing to say about what those nations did to further the collective knowledge of the entire planet, or the advances in technology, medicine and science that system brought about. But, again, the story I'm here to tell is how all that was wrong, misguided, and unnatural. And those that came before The Fall would surely see our traditions and customs as unnatural. Taking newborn children from their mothers and rearing them anonymously in a crèche would sound as alien to them as marriage is to any of those people sitting out there.

But. I am Story and this is my job. To show how wrong we were and how right we are, even well, even if I think differently.

Tonight is a teaching that he's put off telling for many years. It is a long Telling. When he does finally finish, he's exhausted and needs help to get off his chair. One of the older boys in the crèche helps him back to his seat amongst the children, where he rests his head on his walking stick with his breath coming hard and in long, deep draws.

The rest of the night goes by quickly, just a few notices from nearby communes and a brief harvest report from the farm holdings. He gets up and leaves with the children, following them back to the crèche where he keeps his records and a small room with his bed and other personal effects. The records he uses to create his Tellings are made up of stacks of books and bundles of loose notes, the result of years of personal research and investigation. More recently, he has worked with other members of the commune and even other Storys from neighboring communes up and down the coast.

Then there are the secretive records of the commune's crèche. These he keeps the old fashioned way, using machines made before The Fall. His attachment to the crèche is twofold. First, his position requires him to track records of pairings, and the resulting births, which logically would place him physically close to the crèche. Second, the crèche was the only building permitted and allotted use of electricity and that enabled all the communes to keep a small old-fashioned computer handy to keep those records, easily and securely.

"Story!" He recognizes Rebecca's voice right away and keeps walking, slightly picking up the pace over the loose pebble path.

"Story, wait." She catches up to him and puts a light hand on his shoulder. "Story, come tonight and stay with us. Mary promised to be there and her holding just gathered some honey today. I know how you love your tea with honey. Won't you come over?"

Oh, not tonight, not on this night, I couldn't possibly, he wants to say. But he can't say no to her. "Well, I suppose if you have the room…"

"Story, I will always have room for you in my hold. Anyway, a few of the boys will be away with Veronica's men. They're training with the horses starting at first light so they're staying with them, which means I'll have plenty of space. Actually, it will feel empty without them." She lets the silence hang there for a minute.

Ah, of course. Well, now I know why she wants me over. I guess it might be time for her hold to grow some more. We do have several children of age at the crèche. The old man starts counting the children of Rebecca's hold, starting with the oldest boys still living there, holdless as of yet. Then, in his mind he lists the girls still living there.

I wonder, does she want to nominate one of her girls for a holding? It has been several years, at least five, since the last holding was created. For the commune to grow, a new Mother must be named by Story and voted on by the council of Holding Mothers. *Maybe she just wants to move one or two girls out to the crèche. She does have more than average, even for a holding of her size.* The crèche usually needed more girls to help out with the young of the commune. And, truly, not every girl wanted to form a hold of her own. A commune with too many holds couldn't support itself and needed to depend on other communes to survive. That would be unacceptable.

That was tonight's Telling, he thinks to himself. *Unchecked growth and misplaced dependence led to The Fall. All the seemingly powerful nations with their populace crammed into nothing more than over-populated rabbit warrens.*

"Also, Matthew will be there. You know how much he idolizes you." She pauses for a few beats as other groups walk by them, acknowledging Story, exchanging small talk and then continuing on their way with lanterns swaying in their hands. At that moment, Josephine, the commune's senior Mother, spots the pair and makes a quick turn, calling out for the old man.

"Story, I believe that was one of the most emotional Tellings I've ever heard. I must say I was close to tears myself. I don't know how you do it."

"Well, Mother," he says with a sigh, trying to put all his exhaustion into the words, "it is a Telling that does raise some terrible emotions in all of us."

"I must say."

Oh, must you now? The old man thought. *I really have more important things to do than stand here discussing a Telling with you, Mother Josephine.*

"They certainly had some strange customs before The Fall, but I just can't believe that a woman would voluntarily live with a man for life. And raise his offspring. By herself?" She punctuates her words with her usual grunt of disbelief, a sound that Story always found reminiscent of a sow.

"It does sound…unnatural. Doesn't it, Story?" Rebecca picked up where Josephine had left off. "How would two people, alone and busy with their individual communes, ever have the time or the knowledge to raise children outside of a creche?"

Story reflexively shifts into his teaching mode.

"Well, Mother Josephine, they had much smaller creches before, sometimes only two children, even just a single child. I'm sure our system of creches and communes would sound just as foreign to them as their families sound to us."

"Yes. Luckily, I have you, Story. I have you to remind us of those cancers that plagued our ancestors. Those images of the past are just the things we use to scare the children of the creche with." She turns to leave. "Thank you, Story, what a beautiful lesson tonight," she says over her shoulder as she continues to her holdfast.

Eyes averted, feet shuffling, Rebecca picks up where she was before the interruption. "Well, anyway, I think Matthew wants to ask to apprentice with you tonight."

Tired with all of tonight's emotion, it takes him a few minutes to realize what she just said. Lost in thought, he doesn't realize that she has turned him onto the path towards her holdfast. They walk in silence for a few more heartbeats along the pebbles. Their lanterns cast twin yellow beams through the dim evening.

Then he stops and looks up at Rebecca.

"I..." he starts. "I do suppose I am getting along in age." *Am I that old? It has been over sixty years since I was apprenticed to Lorie. That was it, that was her name, the last Story. The one I replaced. The one...that night. It was a Seventh Night then, just like tonight. Too many coincidences. Too old, too old for these emotions.* He starts to shake his head, but his companion presses on.

"He has a good strong voice and has shown some talent with numbers. I don't think you could find anyone else that the children look up to as much as Matthew. He's been staying at the crèche on and off helping with the chores. I hardly see him at the hold much anymore."

It was true; Story had seen the boy more often working at the crèche with the children. He had even heard him doing Tellings of his own design to the older children, Tellings of the heroes of the new beginning. Of Gordon The Planner, Loretta The First Mother, and Great John The Lost.

A new Story. My apprentice. I wonder if Matthew really knows what he's asking for. Being Story for a commune is not all Tellings and birthings and recording numbers and counting seasons. There are hard decisions, and difficult truths. I had hoped my apprentice would have been a girl. It is much easier for them to bear the duties. I should know. The requirements fall more easily on the shoulders of a woman, than a man. Even now.

"Oh, I...I don't know." He has to make her understand that he can't do this right now, not this night. Not now. He stops then, looking up at the moon, the beautiful silvery orb. It just hangs there, a few days after its fullness, illuminating the commune in an even gray light.

Had it been a Full Moon that night as well? It's late into summer. Have the men of Gloria's holdfast started the winter wheat yet? They'll need to get into the field within the week if we are to have a crop to carry us through the snows. The commune has grown since that night long ago.

"Story, we're here," she says softly, drawing him out of his reverie. She looks through the open door into the large hold. "I can see Mary's already at the fire with the kettle on. Everyone is expecting you." She gives his arm a tender squeeze.

He looks up at her, focusing on her eyes. "Do you remember ever hearing tonight's Telling before?" he asks, more urgently than intended.

She looks at him strangely, pauses a few heartbeats before answering. "No, come to think of it, it's a new Telling for me. Why do you ask?"

"How many Seventh Nights do you suppose you've missed?" His voice starts to crack. Emotion flows from him, unwanted.

"Story." She takes his arm and walks a few paces, away from the front door. He sees the concern in her eyes. "Story, you know I've not missed a single Seventh Night since I was given my own hold. It's forbidden of a holding's Mother to miss a Seventh Night. And I've been a Mother for almost forty years now." She smiles softly. "You've been Story for all those years and more. Now that you bring it up, I don't think I've ever heard that Telling before. What do you call it, the Family Telling?"

"Yes, The Family Telling. Every child born in the crèche hears that Telling on their tenth birthday, and at least once every year from that day on until they move onto a holding. It's the most important Telling a Story…" He stops, trying to swallow a lump in his throat that was fighting the words. Trying to silence him. "The most important story I have to tell." He shudders, letting out a long breath.

"But, Story." He sees her genuine concern. "Tonight was the first time any of us have heard that Telling? Why?"

He looks up, trying to find that almost full moon again. But she eludes him. She refuses to offer him any opportunity to distract her, to distract himself. Just the stars are there. The stars and the great Milky Way with all its beautiful colors.

They never saw this, he thinks. *They couldn't have. Not with their cities, not with their lights. If they had, would they have been different? Would they have made the choices we've made? We have almost all their knowledge. And possessing that knowledge, this is the result of the choices we've made. The choices that led us through the ashes, through the sickness and disease, through the Second Age of Darkness to here. Here. But.*

"Because I'm not certain they were all that wrong." There, he said it.

"Story!" Her hands flew up to her face in shock. "How could you say something like that? Not you of all people." Her concern quickly melts away, replaced with something closer to disbelief, almost anger.

"And how could you betray your position? The council will need to hear of this, Story. I do not like the position you've put me in."

He looks back up into her eyes. The sun had set an hour ago, but he didn't need the light to see how green they were, green with those small flecks of gold that catch the light just so. He sees those eyes every morning, staring back at him while he shaves. They are his eyes, and he knows how she has her mother's slender nose and thick dark hair.

Oh, my dear, I haven't even begun.

"I..." His voice cracks. "I have a daughter."

Her anger turns to horror in an instant. He has to keep going. If he falters here he never will get the words out.

"Her name is..."

"Rebecca!" The old man's head snaps around to the open door of the holdfast.

"Rebecca!" Mary calls again. "The tea is ready. You two should come in. It's getting cold."

He grabs Rebecca's hands before she could answer, squeezing them hard and drawing her closer.

"You! You are my daughter." He squeezes her hands even tighter, shaking them as if trying to physically break through all those years of accumulated belief.

"You are my daughter and you have one son and three daughters of your own. Your eldest, Sarah, just gave birth to a beautiful boy. Rebecca, you are a grandmother, and thanks to Loretta, I am a great-grandfather." Rebecca's face is grey-white like ash now. Her hands have gone limp and cold.

"Story. No, that cannot be. The Telling. It was too long. Too emotional for you. You should go. Go back to the crèche and we can talk tomorrow." Her voice is so distant. "You cannot have children. No Story can have children. You cannot, it is forbidden. We—the whole commune—we are your children."

"No, no, Rebecca. I have one child. You."

"No!" She wrenches her hands away from his and stomps her foot down hard in the dirt. "No pairings are created without the consent of the council. No council can approve of a pairing without the consent from their Story. And a Story cannot accept a pairing that would create abomination."

She ticks off the commune's laws to the old man as if he had never heard of them before. But he knew them. He knew them very well. That was why that Seventh Night years and years ago—that Seventh Night he was named the next Story—that Seventh Night he and Rebecca's mother stole out into the night and "paired."

The word tastes like bile. All those emotions, rising, rising now. Having to assist in Rebecca's birth and show no amount of emotion. How could he? It was just the birth of another child at the crèche. He had already witnessed three since becoming Story. Emotion would not have been accepted. It would have been…unnatural.

Then, as if all that was just not enough. He had to watch her mother pass there, in the crèche, the birthing having taken her life. His precious Raicheal, a few short minutes with her daughter was all she had before she was taken. Birth and death within a few hours, and he swallowed his pain, his grief, his loss unable to be expressed once again because it would be…unnatural…to mourn the loss of a member of a commune. Much like birth, death wasn't to be expressed in emotion.

So, he did what would be expected of Story, in truth what would be expected of any member of the commune. He swallowed his joy; he swallowed his grief. And he swore to never speak of the Telling of The Family ever again.

"Stop it!" The old man shouts, spittle and tears mixing together and flying out of his mouth. "This is wrong. We are wrong!"

"How can you say that, Story? How could you, of all people?"

"Rebecca, you were not born because some paperwork said the commune needed another child. Not because some Mother's hold needed a girl to churn butter or weed a field of corn. *As the laws dictate.*" The old man puts all the venom he can muster into these last words. "You were born because your mother, my darling Raicheal and I loved one another. Yes, there was evil before The Fall, the world was full of evil: evil men, evil countries, evil acts and evil beliefs. But it also had love!"

Silence breaks over them. A few beats of his old, lonely heart and he can hear the grass, dry from a too-hot summer, crunch beneath the feet of the children slowly approaching from Rebecca's holdfast. His daughter's house. His eyes begin to water, his voice to waver.

"My name is Michael, and this is my story."

Born in the summer of '69, raised on all things Star Wars, comic book, and British heavy metal, **Butch Kenney** was shuffled around the country and overseas in his childhood. The older of two boys in a military family, he lived in the Midwest and the Southwest for most of his childhood, and then moved to England where he graduated in a Department of Defense High School. Returning to the states to start college, he chose his major most unwisely and ended up back in college ten years later. Now a programmer for a large Midwest medical school, he spends his time writing (programs and fiction), and enjoying life with his wife, five cats and two dogs.

How Frank Delano Changed the World, But Not as Much as He Thought

By
Torrey Podmajersky

"The question is, what kind of adults do we want them to be?" Frank stared at the smoke wisping up from the firepit. "We can have kids—well, you kids can. You will. Heck—it's pretty clear that you are."

Frank glanced at Elle, who blushed and held Malik's hand tighter. She had just started to show—but Frank was sure others were in the same condition.

Frank shook his head. "I'm not here to moralize. You're doing exactly the right thing. Mary and Cameron started even sooner." Frank felt the lump rise in his throat, then drop. Even his grief was exhausted. "But Mary's gone, and Cameron and I will just have to make it. We've got to do it for Emily." He looked at the infant, limp asleep in her father's arms.

"We've got good walls and fences, and we've got food growing. When we fight among ourselves, we don't let it get too bad."

He looked at Cyrus, and then to Mike. The meaning was lost on nobody.

"I don't know how any of you were raised. I don't know if you went to pre-school or had a nanny or got straight-As or if your daddy beat you. And the only reason I might care is how you treat my granddaughter."

"So I called a rules meeting." Frank's gesture wasn't big, but pointed to where the city once stood. "I know most of you liked Mary, and I like to think her mother and I had something to do with that. Well, it wasn't by accident.

"I'm not going to say we should give kids whatever they want. Louis thinks I'm scary and mean, sometimes, and I'm sure I am. But I will never give up on helping him be the best person he can be, because that's what I decided, back when he first found the camp."

Louis built and tumbled towers of gravel as the group sat in the erstwhile parking lot. He perked up when he heard his name, but it was just Frank, just talking, as usual.

"And that's what I want to make into a rule: that parents don't get to quit. You're going to screw up, but you don't get to quit. Any one of you, if you raise a child, will let him down."

Tears ran in the channels down his face, and Frank let them flow. "It means you get to try again, and maybe fail again." Emily stretched, then gave a delicate snore. Her eyes opened as she startled herself awake. Frank reached out to hold his granddaughter.

When he spoke again, his voice was low. "These kids, they didn't see how horrible it was. They haven't seen what we had to do. They'll find out what happened, but they won't have to live through it. Their whole job is to figure out who they are, and then be that. Just by doing that, they'll start a better place than we can make for them.

"I know I'm not going to see it. I'm the oldest person I know, and I was as exposed as anyone.

"When I go, I want to know Emily is safe with you."

Mike shrugged, and took off his hat. "Let's put it to a vote. Louis, time to take the hat around."

Louis's favorite privilege was to carry the hat around the circle as people voted. He held the baseball cap by the brim, open side up.

Mike raised his voice, and addressed the whole circle. "We're going to vote after all. The rule is this: Parents don't get to give up. If it's voted in, we're all bound by it. If the rule is broken, the usual consequence applies." Mike looked at each face. "Hold up your vote, and record it in the hat."

Mike picked up one piece of gravel, held it up to show the group and put it in the hat. As Louis made his way around the circle, each person held up their hand to show their vote.

Louis stopped front of Cyrus, and Frank drew breath between his teeth.

Cyrus held up an empty hand.

"Dammit Cy—" Mike's face darkened, but Cyrus shook his head.

"I'm not voting down." True to his word, he didn't reach into the hat to remove the one or two stones he was allowed. "I'm just not voting." He shrugged. "I'll be good to kids—I'm good to Louis, aren't I?"

Louis nodded, then whirled around, confused at who he should be nodding to.

"I just don't believe in a rule about how we raise them. I know that I—if I'm lucky enough to have children," Cy's ears got red, and he didn't look at any of the women around the circle. "I'm never going to let them down. But Frank—"

He waited until the older man made eye contact.

Cyrus continued, "It's not like someone's stealing food, or any of the other rules. If someone breaks a rule, we kill them. We're all committed to that. I don't see how we can draw that line."

Everyone could hear the tack-tack-tack of rock against rock as Louis jangled the gravel in the cap.

Frank sighed. "I can respect that, Cy. Thank you for not voting down, and thank you for speaking up. But can I ask you a favor?" His voice was soft.

"What is it, Frank?"

"Will you help me and Cameron, while we raise Emily?"

Color rose in Cyrus's neck and face. He cleared his throat. "I'll help—I'll help with Emily. Of course I will."

Frank's head jerked down in a single nod. "Thank you, Cyrus. I knew I could count on you."

Every other person put at least one stone in the cap.

"That's settled, then." Mike said, when the circle was complete. "How many was that, Louis?"

Louis looked up at the sky, and screwed his eyebrows together. "Fifty-four."

"Fifty-four—are you sure?"

"Yup. There are thirty three grownups, and Cy didn't put any in, but he didn't take any out, and everybody else put at least one in, and twenty-two put two in."

Mike emptied the gravel from his hat, and slapped the cap against his thigh to shake off the dust. "So that's our newest rule: Kids come first. Any other new business?"

While nobody responded, Mike put the cap back on his head. "We're done, then."

As the camp moved away from the circle, Louis walked over to where Frank sat with Emily.

"She smells bad," Louis pointed out.

"Good thing I've got one clean diaper left. I'll go washing as soon as she gets some food and goes to sleep again."

"Can I feed her?"

"That would be a big help. Go grab me water bucket, and I'll get her cleaned up first."

As Louis ran off, Frank felt the weariness settle over him. For a moment, he was acutely aware of the way things used to be, the past from which he could never have imagined changing his granddaughter's diaper in the yard of an erstwhile welding and fabrication shop.

As he untied the wrap that held her diaper together, Emily grinned and farted.

Frank smiled back, even as he suffered through.

Torrey Podmajersky

Torrey Podmajersky writes science fiction, fantasy, and stereo instructions for the 21st century. Drawing on experiences in high-tech, small farming, home health care, science education, foster parenting, and corporate communications, her stories confront the darkness in a relentless search for hope. Published work includes the short story "Automatic Selection" and the young adult novel *Gathering Grace*. Torrey lives in Seattle with antique cats, a new-minted adult, freeloading chickens, and a cutler. Follow her adventures at blog.torreybird.com and @torreybird on Twitter.

Jar Washing Day

By
Leslie Light

    Sylvie Mason Crenshaw stood at the edge of her planted terrace, where plants were preparing to set fruit, and looked over the remains of the city. It was early morning and the sun was rising over the crest of the hill behind her. The clear day was a rarity; usually the mornings were fog drenched, and the chance for a view had pulled her to the edge. It was spectacular.

    The cool ocean air ran smoothly over Sylvie's skin, not ruffling the orange skullcap she wore to keep the dirt out of her hair. Her old, red windbreaker snapped in the breeze with a plastic sound.

    "Now how's that for a view?" she asked no one. She was alone on the terrace. Her husband, Tate, wearing his old well-loved undergrad UCLA sweatshirt, had gone to the bottom of the hill to check the grey water tank with Lewis. The rest of the family was off at other tasks.

    Before her stretched the tidal flats of San Francisco Bay, the waves lapping over washed-out streets and against the walls of flooded buildings. A one-foot rise in sea level had moved the water inland by a mile or more in the flood basin. Seaweed floated where lawns had once been; long-legged birds mined worms where there'd once been cars. Sea level rise, earth subsidence, dead water pumps…there were too many reasons for any individual one to matter now. It made her smile—nothing to be done for any of it. Nothing but living left now.

Three children and eleven adults lived on their section of the hill. Sylvie had once wondered out loud how many acres of farming they did. But really, did the number of acres matter if they had enough to eat? And that they had: enough to eat and enough left over to trade for meat and goods when they wanted or needed either. Sylvie was their chief preserver, so she only had one terrace to maintain. Today was too early in the season for preserving; it was a jar washing day.

Looking down at the city from a view she never would have been able to afford before civilization left her behind always brought Sylvie to a thinking mood. And she had plenty to think about; Tate had brought her a choice last night, a choice between breaking up their family and growing it.

She was slowly unspooling it all in her mind, starting, as was right, from the beginning.

* * *

Six years ago, Sylive had asked, "So what's going on?" She had heard the radio announcer's voice in the shower but couldn't make out the words, just the tone. "Is there another riot?"

Tate shook his head and sipped his coffee. "The government has announced an evacuation." He turned up the radio:

> "Given the ongoing state of affairs in California, Nevada, and Oregon, the United States Government will be transporting all American citizens east of the Rocky Mountains, until such time as proper precautions can be taken to defend the lives and property of all Americans."

"What the hell?" she said, slumping into the chair. "They're just going to abandon us? Abandon California?"

"Between the earthquakes and the rising seas, they are having a hell of a time maintaining…well, anything out here," he said and Sylvie had to nod in agreement—even then, her hot shower had been provided by their rainwater tank on the roof and a gas-powered generator in the garage.

"What should we do?" Sylvie asked, her voice a whisper. "We should go…but…living somewhere I don't know doesn't seem any better. I mean, we'll probably end up in a refugee camp."

They both sighed, listened to the radio announcer repeat himself, to people on the street outside their windows start to panic.

"And the time is 9:06 am," the announcer concluded the announcement with the time, all in the same even tone.

"Tate, your phone…" Sylvie reminded him gently, her hand on his arm. "9 to 10, remember?"

"Yeah, yeah," he said with a start, fumbling across the table for his phone. They kept it off most of the time to preserve the battery. It hadn't been on five minutes when it rang—Sylvie could hear Davenport's loud authoritative voice on the other end. Tate nodded, said a few words, hung up.

"We're going down to their place. Pack a bag, we may not be back."

* * *

Pausing from her weeding, Sylvie straightened and stretched her back, returning from the memory. Her muscles strained from the work. She'd led a life of desk-bound nothing for almost twenty years before civilization as she knew it had begun to splinter.

She was glad she only had one terrace to tend, glad that she had accidentally turned up with a usable skill. She'd taken up canning and preserving foods when her grandmother died. Six months after the funeral she missed, she had received in the mail a box full of books and canning supplies with a note: "You're the only one of us we figured would use this. If you put up any peaches in California, send us some. Love."

Even now, from the middle of the terrace looking over the clear blue bay, thinking of her grandmother's put-up peaches brought a lump to Sylvie's throat. She'd learned all she could about the process, preserving everything she could get her hands on with a passion born of a distance she couldn't cross. There was something so permanent in recreating her grandmother's actions, in recreating the actions of those countless women for whom this process had been the difference between a decent winter and a thin one…a starving one.

In the end, this thing she'd taken up out of grief and guilt had maybe saved her life and the lives of those she loved, the family with which she'd chosen to stay behind.

* * *

"So what do we do?" Sylvie asked over her third bottle of Davenport's home-brewed beer. The four of them, she and Tate, Davenport and Manda, sat around Manda's farmhouse-sized kitchen table, watching out of a picture window that overlooked they bay. They could see the city begin to burn in the flatlands as the panic spread.

"I don't want to go," said Manda, "and I've got a basement full of supplies that says I don't have to."

Sylvie blinked, surprised at the steel in Manda's voice. "I don't want to go either. But is that an option—not going?" she looked around, hoping for a sensible response.

Tate shrugged, "Option? Sure, I guess you could put it that way, but the radio says that people will be forcibly evac'd if necessary, so as to preserve 'safety.'" His air-quotes were obvious by the tone of his voice.

"Or property," Manda said, filling in the irony.

"Both," said Davenport, not turning from the window.

"So what do we do?" Sylvie asked again. There was a long silence, then Davenport again.

"I am tired of work; I am tired of building up somebody else's civilization." The other three knew from his tone that he was quoting a poem. Davenport, a literary professor at one of the local junior colleges, was a tall, dark-skinned man with a shaved head and a voice made to read poetry. There was another long moment as they waited for him to explain himself.

"Don't you get it?" he said, turning to look them each in the face. "We've sat around this table and complained about the world for the last five years, at least once a week. We don't like the government, we don't like the rest of the people we're supposedly citizens with, we're fed up with the whole rotten mess called 'civilized living.' This is our chance to get out of the world, to start our own."

Manda nodded, her curly hair bouncing.

"Just on your crawlspace full of food? I don't think so." Tate's sensible nature doubted immediately.

"No, no...we build it, here, on this hill side. Grow our own food, raise produce, do what we have to do. We've been talking about it in small ways since the first quake."

Silence as each of them thought about it.

Manda spoke first. "Maybe it is time to stop talking and start doing. There is plenty of information on how it could be done, in theory. Library's full of books on gardening, building things."

Tate warned, "It really won't be that easy. We'd be flying without a net."

"Sure, but we've already got a good start, I mean, I didn't know anything about water conservation a year ago, but since PG&E went the way of the dinosaur, I've figured it out. It'll be hard, but isn't everything?" Sylvie paused and looked around. She was surprised to see the other three nodding along. "Besides, the Internet is full of articles on self-sufficiency. We just have to download it and print it all before the power goes out for good." She couldn't believe that she was starting to think it was actually possible.

"That's it!" Davenport said, getting more excited. "We're smart people, we know how to follow directions. We collect the data and we do it, right here on the side of this hill, right in this house and in the houses around."

"What about the people in those houses?" Tate asked.

"They're already gone. People with family back East who could take them in have been leaving here for months."

"But...the radio said it was a forcible evacuation," Sylvie countered.

"That's where the crawlspace does come in. We just hide out until they're gone," Davenport said. "We'll be like slaves in an ancient attic or Jews in a long-gone basement. This will be our chance to get free. Really free."

"Just the four of us?"

"No, I'd invite Benjamin and Zia too, they were here at that last dinner party," Davenport smiled. "The one where we made plans for the end of the world."

They all sighed and smiled. It had been a joke then, a drunken party game of What-If. But now, it was real.

Davenport stood up, "But only if we're in, if we're going to give it our best damn try."

"I'm in...I want to try." Sylvie said, standing too. Manda stood with them. Tate looked up, considering.

"If we're going to try, we'll have to be a family in this, all together," Tate said.

"Haven't we always been?" Davenport offered Tate his hand. Tate took his friend's hand automatically, then stood.

* * *

It wasn't even a whole day before the six of them were sitting around the table, listing the work and getting ready to work the list.

Their group was small: Sylvie and Tate; Manda, who grew food, and Davenport, who watched the kids. Zia was the genius behind their water system, and her husband Benji managed market days and kept count of the value of things they were pulling out of the ground. They were parents of Effie, the sweetest six-year-old you'd ever want to meet. Proctor was the engineer, she kept track of the buildings and the support walls for the terraces, and Dette was her wife, a great all-around hand. Neighbors of Manda and Davenport, they were the last couple to join. Together, they'd adopted Willis, a pudgy boy of seven who was definitely lucky to have them. Luckier, and better off with two women who wanted him than with whoever his real parents were; they had left him behind to wait for an evacuation bus that wasn't coming.

They acquired two single men too: Lewis and Myers. Sylvie was nervous about accepting unattached men into their little family group. She had some ancient, inexplicable prejudice against any man without a woman to vouch for him. But they needed the muscle, and they'd have their own house, so she wouldn't have to look after them.

Even after she'd been convinced, she still was hesitant to be alone with either of them. She and Zia both held themselves apart, a distance that Lewis and Myers respected. Single men and married women didn't mingle. How strange that those old habits had returned like a dew out of damp ground.

The first year passed amazingly well. A new hand, Ray, joined up to help out when Dette was too sick to help with the harvest. He'd brought rabbits and knowledge of first aid. Life hummed along, complete with the regular fights and trials of community life.

Things changed the winter Sylvie had Georgia. Sometime, somehow in that first frantic postpartum month, Tate fell and broke his arm badly enough that the bone had punctured his skin. He had to go to the doctor. Ray knew of one, but she was the better part of a half day's walk away.

Dette and Ray had led Tate through the fog and misty rain. Dette carried two live rabbits and several jars of potatoes to try to trade for whatever medical attention they could find.

Sylvie was left alone, terrified, exhausted. Myers stayed with her. He knew something of children, he maintained, having raised more siblings than he ever named. They'd been close since then, she and Myers. Was that four years ago? It was. Tate had been gone a week or more on the mend and returned to hold his daughter with his good arm and thank Myers with his broken one.

* * *

Finishing the field, Sylvie had to admit that it had started then, years ago. Through the tricks of fate, she had found herself crying tears of joy over her first daughter's actions onto a shoulder that wasn't her husband's. After that, last night's conversation shouldn't have surprised her, but it had.

She loaded herself up with two bags, one of soap and rags, one of dirty canning jars needing to be cleaned, and thought back over that conversation with a mixture of awe and skepticism, the choices laid out before her beyond what she would ever have thought possible.

Sylvie clanked as she walked, steadily climbing the slightly meandering path up to the wash water shed. She set her load on the washing tables and paused at something missing. The dirty jars were all there in the plastic trays that Dette used to carry them. One even had the usual flyer stuck in it from the Back to America people who were trying to get a caravan of folks together to walk back east.

She pulled out the slip of paper, blue, looked over the hand-scrawled red ink note, not really reading it, but simply taking it in. Taking a moment to consider that whoever wrote this letter cared enough to go back East, but not enough to go alone. Cared enough to have evaded the Feds but not enough to remain. Cared enough to spend their time writing this same note over and over and keep passing it out at the market.

The balance of energy there seemed skewed. Gone were the days when Sylvie did anything that didn't make her happy or make her fed. She wondered which appetite the patriotic writer satisfied with his or her notes: the belly or the mind.

A rustle in the trees reminded her of what was missing. She looked up, expecting to see Myers push through the bamboo like he usually did, come to help her clean and dry the jars. His wide, freckled face splitting into a grin when he saw her, his self-trimmed brown hair bouncing absurdly on his head. He'd admitted to her, one day when they were drying jars in the shed, that seeing her always made him smile, no matter the day he was having. But it wasn't him. It was just the wind making the bamboo leaves sing. They'd agreed that he wouldn't come today. She needed some time to think about what was going on, to make up her mind about some things.

Sylvie carefully loaded the dirty jars into the basin built into the washing table. As she loaded, she counted and as she counted, she replayed the night before in her head.

* * *

"Sylvia," Tate's voice was husky, sleep-laden, but clear in the darkness from over her shoulder. They'd just finished making love and were spooned intimately together in their giant bed. "Sylvia, honest question time."

"Honest question time," she repeated. They had a deal, had kept it from the day they were married ten years before, that after making love, each could ask the other one question and get a completely honest answer. A no-holds-barred straight answer. It was a hard deal, but it represented a space in their relationship where they were always real with each other.

"Sylvia, do you want more children? To have more children?"

Georgia was almost four years old and there had been no new baby, despite their healthy sex life, which wasn't a surprise. When they'd married, Sylvie and Tate had visited a fertility counselor, only to find out that Tate's count was so low that they could skip birth control all together. And they had. They'd been married for six years without any hint of pregnancy before Georgia had come along. She'd been the surprise.

Sylvie took a deep breath and looked out into the darkness of their bedroom.

"I do. Ever since Georgia was born, I've wanted one," she had to stop, collect her thoughts and struggle for that honesty she'd promised her husband. "Georgia completes a cycle for me. She makes things that seemed so odd suddenly seem so right. I understand my mother, finally. I understand planting things and growing things. It's not that life was senseless before, it is just that now, with a baby…children…it makes sense. I do wish I could, but," the wistful tone of her voice hung in the cool air, turning her last word into a sigh.

"Nothing to be done for it," she'd said finally.

"Really? Nothing?" Tate repeated, his voice almost a whisper. Sylvie made a face out of habit.

"What are you getting at, Tate? What's on your mind?" Her tone became serious since she felt teased.

"What if there was something to be done for it. What if you didn't just have to wish any more?"

Sylvie rolled over to face him, eyes straining to see his face close to hers in the darkness. "Tate," she said with a warning in her voice, "don't play games with me, what if what?"

"The other night, while you were out with Dette, Myers was over, helping me with Georgia and we got to talking. He's thinking of leaving the family."

The thought of Myers leaving bent her heart so hard she'd made a noise of protest that ended with a long, scared NO. Sylvie could hear Tate smile in the dark.

"You like him…quite a bit. We both do," he sighed and admitted, "I'd thought when this whole thing started that me and Dav'd be tight forever, but really, as time passes, it is Myers I go to."

She nodded her agreement. "He was there for me. He's always there for me," Sylvie said, choking down a tangle of emotions she was glad her husband couldn't see in the dark. "Why? Why would he go?"

"He wants children, a house full of them. And there isn't anyone here for him to have them with. He's willing to leave, take his chance to go and meet someone."

"He could meet someone? Go and come back?"

Tate shrugged, shifting the bed with his shoulders. "And what if she didn't get on with everyone else? What if she didn't want to join up?"

"What if…" Sylvie repeated, but she had no answer to that question. Tate did.

"But what if he didn't have to go? What if he could have a family, children of his own, here? That'd be pretty…"

Finding Home

"Perfect." Sylvie interjected. There was silence in their room, just breathing and the spring wind outside the windows. Sylvie finally sat up, letting the sheet fall to her lap. In the old world, she'd have turned on the light, but now that was a production requiring fire or the generator. Instead, she just turned and really looked at him, making out the line of his strong nose in the pale light, waiting to watch his lips move. "Tate, what do these two things have to do with each other? Me and children and Myers and leaving?"

"Do you really not get it, Sylvia, or do you just not want to get it."

She stuttered. She did get it, more and more with every passing breath, and it was very quickly tearing her in two. "I'm not going to jump to conclusions on this, you're going to have to say. Honesty time goes both ways." She made her most serious face but had to trust that he could hear what she was feeling.

"Sylvia, Myers and I talked the other night about you having his children."

Even the wind seemed to stop.

"Tate…that's…me and Myers…the old fashioned way?" It was all Sylvie could think of in that flash of a moment, her and Myers the old fashioned way. The thought gave her a flame deep in her belly that immediately drowned in the guilt her conscience poured on it. She covered that guilt with outrage. "How can you even suggest such a thing!"

Tate propped himself up onto his elbows and laughed at her, a hearty genuine laugh. "Sylvia, stop being so full of shit. You'd fuck Myers in a heartbeat."

Sylvie gasped. "How can you even…"

"Like I just did, Sylvia. I'd have to be blind to not see the way you talk to him, touch his arm over dinner."

"I've never, ever been unfaithful to you, Tate. Not for one second," her voice trembled on the edge of tears, realizing how obvious she must have been while also being genuinely hurt.

"I didn't say you had. I didn't say you would. I only said if you weren't married to me then it is pretty obvious how things would be going down right now."

"That's not fair, not a fair question."

"It isn't a question, it is true. If we weren't married, you and Myers..."

"He's not my type."

"The hell you say!" She was shaking so hard that she couldn't even respond.

Tate softened his voice, feeling his wife's tense posture, hearing her breath rattle in her chest as if she were about to cry. "Sylvia, I trust you. I love you. I'm not accusing you of anything. I'm just telling you what I know."

"And what do you know?"

"I know that Myers is my closest friend. I know you're fond of Myers and he's admitted to me on multiple occasions that he's fond of you. Go ahead and pretend you didn't know," he dared her. She finally had to hang her head.

"I know. He told me, years ago. That he...that he had a crush on me. But I didn't think anything of it."

"Right. A crush that hasn't ever gone away. So I know that you two are attracted to each other and get along well together. And I know that he's about the best guy I could ask to have around ever. And I know that the two of you want to have children. The only thing stopping both of you from having children together is me."

"And my wedding vows. Which I take very seriously," Sylvie said in a warning tone.

"I'm not talking about you breaking our wedding vows. I'm talking about changing them to fit the new situation we've found ourselves in."

Sylvie took a deep breath. Tate reached for her, pulling her back down to lay her head on his chest. "Think about it, Sylvia, really think about it. I'd love to have more children too. Let's have what we want, not just what we've been given. Let's have it all. Finally, once and for permanent."

* * *

Sylvie opened the sluice on the basin, bringing in the rush of sun-warmed water from the tank built into the top of the wash water shed, swamping and filling the jars.

While they soaked, she used a handful of kindling to light the rocket stove, a small contraption under the basin that would quickly heat the water hot enough to wash with. Tate's words from last night rang in her ears over the whoosh of the flame catching the wood alight. All.

She moved one step down the table. It was set on a slight angle so the water would run down it, to the next basin, which she filled with the same lukewarm water for rinsing. Water warm, rinse water ready, Sylvie pulled out her rag and soap and set to work on the jars.

Sylvie let the shock of the temperature change mix with the shock she'd felt last night. Yes, she wanted children. Yes, she thought Myers would make a fine father and a fine partner. Yes, the three of them together could support and provide for as many children as she saw fit to carry.

She used the rough, soapy rag to release the built-up sugars and salts in the bottoms of the jars, then she set them back in the water to soak some more. Damn it, if she didn't love Tate, and love him all the more for his honesty. And for the fact that he demanded hers. She looked up from the water, set more jars on the counter and stared across the empty expanse that used to be a road and down the hillside. The only no was the weight of her wedding ring on her left hand and an old, old habit that she couldn't shake.

The stubbornly filthy ones she let sit in the hot water, where a gentle steam rose. It seemed unthinkable, bringing Myers to their bed, but it was sensible. And Tate's idea. And still wrong.

Sylvie set to scrubbing the remaining jars briskly now, shaking them, not paying attention to their clanking together or to how hot the water had gotten. What would she tell Georgia, about the father of her siblings? What would they tell the rest of the family about Myers moving in? How would she reconcile the guilt that having another child was more important to her than keeping to her marriage vows? Was it that simple, a matter of her selfish desire outweighing all else?

At the same time, what vow was she breaking? What sin was there in their mutual desire, all three of theirs, to have something that fate had conspired to keep them from? And was not fate now just as swiftly and randomly conspiring to allow them all to succeed? What were her other options? This hole in her belly where a baby should go; Tate forever sorry for something he could never fix; Myers gone. No one getting what they wanted, only what they thought they should have.

She scrubbed frantically now at the last jar, the caked-on food stubborn beyond reason, the water all but boiling around her fingers, her mind racing. There were so many questions and each dragged up a harder answer, a deeper demand for her honesty.

Yes, she desired him. Yes, the idea of having so much support and love around her and her children thrilled her. Yes, they could be happy together. The old world was gone, civilization having retreated eastward, but it lingered around them. They grew their own food, ate what they wanted as they wanted. They invented and imagined and took time to do nothing at all at a rate that made their old lives look like slave labor in comparison.

What were they doing, if not building their own world? What was the point of letting the last bus leave without them, if not to be happy? Was she not finally free to do that? To be happy? Weren't they all?

Finally, she pulled her hands out of the water, shaking them to release the heat from her fingertips. Then Sylvie plunged them into the cooler water, which felt freezing in comparison and pulled from her a cry that faded into a long scared Yes. She just stood with her hands flat on the damp counter, letting all the questions and answers fade out with the burning in her hands. They were raw and shaking, her fingers, and distant through the cloud of tears that had only just started to drain down her cheeks.

"I am tired of life, I am tired of building up someone else's civilization. Let us build our own."

Sylvie kicked out the small fire with the toe of her boot, grinding down till the embers were dead. Then she dug a larger stick from the kindling pile and used it to fish the last jar out of the hot water. It was still dirty, stained from storing some long-gone thing.

Using the stick as a lever, she chucked the jar as hard as she could into the remnants of the road, watching it shatter against a corner of concrete, the glass pluming up, then showering down in a sparkle in the sunlight. She arrayed the now-clean jars in the sunny corner of the wash shed table and opened the plug at the bottom of the rinse basin, allowing both basins to drain down to the willow tree that shaded the table and chairs where she and Myers used to pass the time while waiting for the jars to dry.

Not today, though, there was too much else to do. There were more questions to be asked and answered. Would there be promises and vows? New names and new decisions? What would this new world look like, the world that they were going to build?

Yes, they were going to try to build it. Going east was not an option, neither in their lives or in their heads. Yes, they would preserve the best things, keep the old promises. They had to sort the good from the bad, letting the useless break and fall away, liberating the best parts, cracking the pavement and letting the vines grow wild over the old curbs.

Yes, it would be a lot of work. Yes, they were going to be happy.

Sylvie left the jars and wet rags on the table to dry alone, gathered up her empty bags and soap. It was almost lunchtime. If she hurried, she could meet Davenport when he was taking the kids out to forage through the areas of their territory where the first fruits were ripening. Maybe there'd be berries for dessert tonight with Tate and Georgia. They could discuss, explore, and decide, going into the unknown as they always had: together.

And tomorrow, with ripening berries and clean jars, jam wasn't far behind.

Leslie E.H. Light is a life-long writer, though this is her first published short story. The theme connecting all of her writings, ranging from historical fiction to modern dark fantasy to cyberpunk, is a belief in the inherent magic of mundane life.

Surrounded by the sort of people who turn up in historical documentaries, Leslie could adequately dress herself in the style of any time period from 900BCE to 2900CE. Born in Cleveland, Ohio, Leslie now lives happily in the San Francisco Bay Area where she works as an editor for non-profit organizations. Prepared for the inevitable apocalypse, she's already found the house she'll move her family into and updates the list of who she'll bring with her on a regular basis.

Leslie would like to thank the East Bay Writer's Collective and her own personal writing Jedi for their feedback and support. And of course, her husband and new baby girl: this future I write—it is for us.

Lunation: An Aperitif
By
Michaela Hutfles

    Surviving alone was lonely, it held no future.
    By then, the bullets had run out, were saved for hunting or owned by those who were dug in too deep and not going anywhere. The smoke from small fires could be seen in the distance on full moon nights. Five years ago ago, that would have been careless, incompetent, asking for trouble. At first, it was infrequent—in the spring, in the fall, height of summer, depth of winter; occasional plumes of white pope selecting smoke appeared. Daring plumes declaring, "Here I am, come and join me."
    They started to arrive: onesy, twosy, all cautious and curious.
    They all brought strange gifts for surviving, items no one from before would have known were needed. The Storyteller who could remember for days; he knew *Beowulf* and the Mabinogion, the *Honeymooners* and understood the plot of *Lost*.

Finding Home

The Doctor, who wasn't really, but somehow everyone who came to see her went away healed in some way.

The Judge was fair in ways no one disputed or grumbled over; he treated everyone with all the love he had used previously for his lost grandchildren.

The Victorians, siblings with nothing in common from the time before but blood, a love of house plants, and a sourdough starter. Now, together, they shared delicate tasks in then greenhouse, a dance of pollen and potential; holding together thin panes of glass with the hope that the surviving cacao and dwarf tangerine might fruit one more time through the magic of heated beds and perhaps even a prayer or two.

The Warrior, who couldn't talk anymore, not about any of it—in part due to the night terror, screaming herself hoarse. She brought more of what everyone wanted and feared the most; she brought others. When the moon was full, if there was smoke between hearth and horizon, she would find them and in wordless ways invite them to join, to trade, to share or to stay away. Perhaps they should have called her The Diplomat, but even in one of the havens of new civilization some scars were too deep to ignore, for all of them.

Together, they built again, each with their small, unexpected gifts.

One of them had been raising purple cabbages, a welcome change from the green many others had raised during the isolation. Between them, there were three varieties of potatoes, a bounty no one had expected to ever see again.

A scrawny slip of a girl had been secretly sharing her food with a pair of ducks. She finally had to tell her mother when they prepared to move. She didn't want to leave her friends behind, so her mother caught them and everyone profited with eggs.

An unsuspected goatherd arrived and—better still—their human knew how to spin their cashmere hair.

Unforeseen losses came too. With no weathermen to predict, the floods nearly washed away everything, but hope was more buoyant when all of them hoped together. They recovered what they could, moved to higher ground and tried not to starve.

The year the duck girl died was hard for all of them; she had never known a vaccination's sting and diseases both old and new had come to call. When the Storyteller's son was born blind he was destined to learn his father's craft. The Victorians promised to teach the boy where every bench was, and the feel of every seed and leaf and stem.

    Eventually, The Judge passed and all were lost for a while.

    And life went on, as it always had, as it always would. With people finding each other in a wilderness.

About Timid Pirate Publishing

Timid Pirate Publishing believes that heroes walk among us, although most don't wear capes. You never know when your own inner hero will awaken. We believe that joy and inspiration are everywhere, and once found, should be shared. To that end, we find stories that inspire and delight, and that broaden the worlds of possibility. In short: Adventures Unlimited.

Timid Pirate Publishing provides free, original stories at www.timidpirate.com, along with the Parsec award-winning audio drama "Cobalt City: Adventures Unlimited."

Keep in touch

Find us on Twitter @TimidPirate, "like" us on Facebook, or subscribe to our monthly newsletter for all the news and updates on coming projects, appearances, and special events.

Forthcoming

In 2012, keep an eye out for our forthcoming trilogy of super-hero Young Adult novels and two exciting super-hero novellas.

The third season of our 2011 Parsec Award-winning podcast, "Cobalt City: Adventures Unlimited," concludes this winter.

CPSIA information can be obtained at www.ICGtesting.com
Printed in the USA
LVOW092128301111
257283LV00002B/1/P